Katie's Server

Sisters of Annis Novellas

PGDevlim

Published by PGDevlim, 2023.

This is a work of fiction. Similarities to real people, places, or events are entirely coincidental.

KATIE'S SERVER

First edition. March 30, 2023.

Copyright © 2023 PGDevlim.

ISBN: 979-8224494231

Written by PGDevlim.

Sisters of Annis
Katie's Server

Chapter One

Katie felt like a queen. Plush, plump pillows cushioned her head as she lay back on the double bed. Her slender legs were draped over the side, parted for the young man who knelt between them. Naked and hard, as she liked her unlocked boys, he traced tender kisses over her soft curves, trailing from foot to knee, then higher, slipping over her thigh towards the heat between her legs. The intimate contact felt like a blessing from an angel performing benediction over her impatient body.

A smile warmed her pale face, alleviating the severity of the dark lipstick and black eye shadow, bringing a cold fury to the dark-haired beauty. Her whispered words of encouragement betrayed a fading Russian accent. "That feels nice."

His lips answered, teasing a pattern of soft caresses over the curve of her thigh, moving closer to the lining of her black, lace briefs.

Katie murmured her encouragement, her hips rising to meet the gratifying touch of his mouth. Her reaction caused him to withdraw, denying her the attention she craved. Cultivating her desire, his firm lips then pressed against her exposed flesh.

Her body surged beneath him. She could feel his rigid cock nudging against her thigh. She wanted to hold him, feel him slide into her, slowly, deeply. Then hard and fast. *Another time*, she thought, denying herself. *He still has to prove himself.*

He caught the summit of her breast in his mouth, his tongue stroking slowly over her nipple. A flick, a pause, then another flick, another pause. His lips replaced his tongue, they locked over her and drew away pulling the peak with them, until he released her with a mischievous smile.

Katie's breath became shallow. Her arms wrapped around his shoulders, long fingernails grazing jet streams down his back. She felt his hand run gently over her thigh, his fingers tip-toeing over her fiery flesh. He slowed as his fingers connected with lace, then gently brushed his thumb over her pussy.

Katie thrust herself upwards. His hand retreated, running up and over her hip before sliding behind her. He lifted her up, squeezed her ass and pulled her against him. His cock nudged her again, probing, yet frustrated by cotton.

Her full lips locked onto his, her tongue brushing and caressing, twirling around then withdrawing. She wanted more, wanted his mouth on the heat between her legs, his kisses against the smooth lips of her pussy, his tongue running over her clit.

Her hands clasped his cock, encouraging its life-giving heat with long, eager movements as she worked his foreskin up and over its bulging head.

He issued a low, bestial groan, then reluctantly pulled away.

Katie's grin exposed her fangs. "Good boy."

He smiled, slipped her briefs over her hips and down her legs, and cast them to the floor beside her discarded stockings, garter belt and brassiere.

"Mmm!" Katie gasped as his lips returned to her breasts. His gentle kisses were interspersed by a skimming tongue that brushed eagerly against her rigid nipples. His touch shooting waves of pleasure through her eager flesh.

Gradually, his focus wound its way down her body. His scant kisses compelled her hips to rise again as her body writhed beneath him. He ignored her invitation, offering light touches that circled her stomach, before slipping over her hip and down onto her thigh.

His mouth teased inwards, skimming the side of her pussy, circling upwards, over her shaven slit, then down the other side. His gentle touch manifested a labyrinth of pleasure throughout her mind. Her flesh was on fire. Every fibre sparking as though a galaxy of suns were erupting through the cosmos of her body.

His tongue brushed against her clit, idly stroking before circling and withdrawing to tease over her wet lips. He kissed her smooth flesh, sliding over her labia, then paused at her entrance.

She shuddered involuntarily, then caught her breath in an attempt to savour every moment. Her fingers twisted through the strands of his light brown hair, forcing his face into her. His tongue flattened, sliding over her wet lips in long, slow strokes before circling around the hood of her clit.

Katie's protracted gasp filled the room, fading gradually as she succumbed to the surging pleasure. She drew a hand to her mouth and bit down on a solitary digit. A trickle of blood oozed from her finger, warm and refreshing, mimicking the wetness between her legs.

He didn't let up, working delicately but rapidly against her. His tongue thrust glancing blows of delight over her pussy, brushing around her clit in tight, evocative circles.

"Yes," she cried, kicking her legs up and over his shoulders. Her thighs tightened around him, locking his face against her.

His tongue worked faster, becoming an instrument of sensual torment. Each stroke felt like a recitation of poetry, each brush an artistic expression of indulgence. Her body became a feather of delight, floating in a dream of desire and sensuality.

The delightful sensations charged through her being. Her back arched, hips bucked against the caresses of his tongue, lapping at her juices, teasing and stroking her clit, again and again and again, before driving downwards to slide against her entrance.

Katie's murmurs became gasps—gasps that transformed into loud, unrestrained moans conducted by each brush of his tongue. Tingles spiralled up through her belly, rocketing to her chest, then higher to permeate into the depths of her mind. She pushed him away as the first tremble swept through her. It sparked every cell, pleasured every nerve, energised every muscle. Her undead soul soared, gliding across orgasmic skies of dreamy energy. Her hands clenched the sateen sheet as her body shuddered beneath pleasurable waves. Gradually they subsided, leaving her gazing absently at the patterned ceiling, her body nourished by the afterglow of her orgasm.

"I hope it was nice, Miss," he said, still kneeling before her.

Katie patted his head and smiled. "You are a very good boy."

He bit his lip, uncertain if he should ask. His stiff cock, rigid with overwhelming desire, forced him to speak. "May I?"

"May you what?" Katie queried, repositioning herself on the bed to lean against the thick, soft pillows that rested against the headboard. She pulled the covers over her lithe, naked body.

"Please, Miss?" He stood, naked and hard before her, a forlorn look of desperation on his face.

Katie repressed a smile. His swollen cock looked impatiently desperate for release. "May you what?"

"Please, Miss, may I be allowed to cum?"

"Cum? Why?"

"Miss?"

"I asked you a question." She felt good; noble, royal, powerful. A woman that had her desires fulfilled by a young man driven by his own desires to satisfy her.

He swallowed. "I hope I have pleased you, Miss. I thought you might... er, you might..."

Katie's response was sharp like a slap across the face. "I might what?"

He choked on his words, as though he were about to cry. "I... I... I thought you might let me cum today."

"How long has it been?"

He gasped and looked down at himself. His response was cautious and tight. "A month."

Katie felt her undead heart thump harder. It wasn't sympathy; it was simply a reflection of how much she enjoyed this power over boys, especially when they were begging to be allowed to touch themselves. It was a potent drug that fed another part of her. "A month? Is that all?"

His fingers rubbed against his thumbs as he did his best to persuade her. "It's a long time for me, Miss."

"No."

His face dropped like a grounded teenager.

"I prefer you like this," Katie said. "I like you hard and horny for me. Now, roll me a spliff."

"Yes, Miss." His shoulders slumped as he walked over to the vanity, his defiantly hard cock leading the way. He glanced nervously at the pink cock cage. It sat there, ready to be worn over his member, like a suit of armour beside her rolling gear and a small bucket of half-melted ice.

"Oh, and put your chastity cage back on."

His heart skipped a beat.

She stared at him through ice-cold eyes, knowing instinctively what he wanted; the caveman instinct that would return him to her. He would lift her up and thrust his cock deep into her hot, wet pussy. His balls would slam against her as he pounded into her, hard and fast, again and again, sliding deep, filling and satisfying her until he exploded, shooting hot jets of cum deep inside her.

His eyes darted anxiously away. "Miss?" he said in a voice that betrayed his fear.

She knew he hoped for the opposite. He was too horny to be frustrated now, but that was half the fun for her. The other side of the coin was the incredible power she wielded when he was locked in chastity. "Jack."

Jack glanced sheepishly at her. The sheet was lower now, exposing her pert, firm breasts as she replaced the necklace upon which his key hung. The key to the padlock. The padlock to his cock cage. The cock cage she wanted him to wear again. He swallowed.

"Do you wish that you had never fallen for me?" she asked. "Never ventured into the club. Never played my game and never agreed to lock yourself up for me."

Jack swallowed again and took a deep agitated breath. "No, Miss," he said. "Thank you for accepting me."

"Put your cock cage on. Now."

His lips tightened, along with his chest and shoulders. "Please, Miss Katie, I'm so horny."

"*Khvatit! Ne prosi.*"

He shook his head. "Sorry, Miss, I don't understand?"

"I said, 'enough, I'm not interested'. And don't beg! Now, put it back on and roll me a spliff." Her eyes narrowed. "Now!"

"Katie," a female voice said from beyond the door.

Katie took a deep breath. Her eyes remained on the forlorn young man. "Just a minute, Emma."

"He's on his way."

"Good," Katie replied. "The spliff can wait. The cage cannot." She was up and beside the en-suite door before he'd even picked it up. "Now, lock yourself up."

He looked lost—lost and confused and that made Katie feel even more powerful. For he would do anything she asked just to earn the right to empty his balls. It made him vulnerable and turned her into a Queen. He would give her money. He would humiliate himself. He would even let her drink his blood. All to achieve a momentary orgasm. An orgasm, if it were permitted, that would quickly pass. His balls would fill again and that natural desire for release would slowly turn volcanic, threatening to drive him crazy with desire, unless Katie granted him the pleasure he sought or directed him to more beneficial ways of self-expression. She had yet to train him properly, teach him how to redirect his desire that, in turn, would fuel his blood.

"Do you understand, Jack?" Katie asked again.

"Yes, Miss," her lost puppy acknowledged.

"Go on then." She watched as Jack's prick remained stubbornly erect. Pointing hard at a strong angle. His balls tightly snuck beneath his shaft. When it failed to subside, he took a deep, preparatory breath and shoved his swollen dick into the bucket of ice. Beneath the sharp, cold shock, he withered quickly. Reluctantly, he forced himself into the cock cage.

"Good boy," she said, and disappeared into the bathroom where the shower burst into life.

She heard the door open and close and she smiled to herself, knowing that another boy had left with blue balls after satisfying his mistress. *And now for the server,* she thought, wondering if the new boy would work out. *As long as he isn't as bad as the last one.* Her mind wandered back to the sour taste of his blood as she drained the life from him.

Chapter Two

Kurt cupped his hands to the cold window and stared out into the gnawing darkness. "Where are we?" As far as he was concerned, they were lost. They'd been driving for an hour and a half and had finally stopped in the middle of nowhere. The driver had already killed the engine and lights, leaving Kurt seated in the pitch black rear of the taxi.

"We're here," the man said, not bothering to turn around.

"I can't see anything."

The driver's sigh sounded closer to a hiss and did little to conceal his irritation. "That's because we're in the middle of the bloody woods. You get out here."

"Can I have my phone back?" Kurt asked, unable to distinguish anything outside the vehicle.

"Weren't you listening? You were told it stays at the office until after the interview."

"But I can't see anything."

The driver shook his head and sighed again. "That's the point."

"Where is the house... exactly?"

"On the other side of the woods. Over the stile."

"I can't see a stile."

"It's on the right."

Gradually, adjusting to the dark, Kurt was able to disassemble trunks and branches from the obsidian swamp of night. They looked like arteries frozen grey by the passing gaze of a vengeful gorgon. An old wooden stile, almost lost to a mass of dead vegetation, waited on the right like a step to the gallows. "I can't see a house."

The driver's response excelled as a tired and well-worn script. "Over the stile, through the woods, over the stile, across the field, over the stile."

"Through the woods?"

"Through the woods."

An unappetising lump sunk to the bottom of Kurt's stomach. It sat there like a brooding ogre sapping his courage and evoking a memory of his fiancée, Tanya. He pushed her image away. "How deep are the woods?" he asked, uncertain if he wanted an honest answer. Inside, the ogre urged him to change his mind. *Don't leave the car,* it suggested. *You'll fail this one too. Just like you failed her. She's better off without you anyway. Wherever she is. Dead, or alive. What are you going to say when you see her? You'll just avoid her again. Avoid her pain. Your pain. Don't make the same mistake twice. Keep the driver talking. Tell him to take you home. You fucked up. She's gone...*

The man's voice drove a stake through the ogre's persuasive words. "Just get out, will you? They're just woods."

"Why can't you take me straight to her house?"

"Look, you either want the job or you don't. I don't care. If you do, get out. If you don't, I'm going."

Kurt stared into the blackness once more. The ogre remained heavy, anchoring him to his seat. "You really don't have my phone?"

Another irritable sigh preceded the driver's answer. "I already told you. It's back at the office. You get it back after the interview—as you've already been told —when I drop you off, back in town."

"Great. Thanks," Kurt said and got out. The ogre dissipated, replaced by a blast of cold air that wrapped around him like a morbid shroud. His first step was into an icy puddle. The freezing water flooded his Oxford captoes, swamping his sock and shooting a shivering chill up his leg. "Damn it!" he exclaimed. He closed the door, steadied himself against the taxi, then stretched wide with his other leg and stepped over the black mirror onto firmer ground. It squelched a warning beneath his feet, and he tiptoed hurriedly across the quagmire, grateful to reach the undergrowth.

The driver gunned the engine, causing the wheels to spin and coat Kurt's legs with slimy clumps of oozing brown sludge as he sped off. *Bastard!* Kurt thought, watching the lights glow infernally as the car disappeared around the corner. It made its way downhill, a wall of light highlighting ghostly treetops before only the sound of its fading engine indicated its waning presence.

Why the hell couldn't he drop me off at the front door, like people do in a normal interview? He felt the ogre tug on his stomach once more. He pushed it away, repressing any subconscious fears provoked by the nightside of nature, and hurried over to the stile. He was up and over, just managing to avoid a second puddle that waited like a trapdoor to another world. He stopped. "Shit!" he said. "I can't see a thing."

His night sight failed him in the woods. The obsidian swamp returned, obliterating definitions of trunks, branches, and viciously spiked brambles. He glanced at the road; at least he could see that, though it was vague and shadowy. But before him there was nothing. Just a wall of black and a chill that seemed to have snuck up and dug deep claws into his body. Kurt pulled his suit lapels over his shirt in an attempt to retain some heat. *I should've worn a coat.*

His stomach felt heavy again, weighted by haunting memories of Tanya's disappearance; from the moment he had discovered she was missing to the sinking reality that she was not going to return as her absence stretched from days into weeks and then months. He rejected the solemn reminders and cautiously moved further into the woods.

There was an elasticity to the ground. It felt soft and almost comforting, a welcome alternative to the quagmire he'd first encountered. Arms outstretched, he shuffled blindly into the smothering blackness. He managed three baby steps before a rough branch struck his head, while another tugged violently at his hair. He gasped, as much in shock as in pain, and twisted in an attempt to free himself. As he turned, another branch stabbed him beneath the ribs. *For fuck's sake, what kind of interview is this? Miss Zharkova's either a sadist or has a twisted sense of humour.*

Cautiously, he backtracked to the centre of the path, then continued, arms raised before him in an attempt to parry blows when he strayed too far to either side. Every now and then he stopped and tried to see through the oily night. It failed to surrender its secrets, and he had to content himself with taking slow, careful steps through the seemingly impenetrable abyss.

He wasn't certain how long it was before a slender gap appeared in the darkness. Trees broke apart creating the semblance of an exit. The lump in his stomach lightened as he saw the stile, and he hurried on, catching a final slap across the forehead from a long, thin branch. "Fuck," he swore, and rubbed his forehead. *I'm going to look like a right idiot,* he thought, hoping the branches wouldn't leave any noticeable marks. He leapt the steps and dropped down onto the grassy field beyond.

He breathed a sigh of relief as he purged himself of the malignant presence that had slunk back into his stomach. There was still no sign of the house. He brushed himself down as best he could while avoiding his mud-stained trousers, and wiped his shoes on the long grass. Hopefully, they would let him clean himself properly; he'd never had to undertake a route march before an interview. This was a first and would be one to share with close friends – if there were any. Tanya would have laughed. In happier times she'd have joined him in the shower, too, at least once he was reasonably clean. He pushed her image away, only far enough for it to remain on the outskirts of his mind, the place where it always lingered.

It was an uphill climb across the field, not steep, but noticeable by the strain on his legs. He moved quickly, then slipped after a couple of steps and went down. His right hand hit something thick and wet and he groaned as he realised what it was. He didn't want to look to confirm his suspicions. It felt gooey, smelt bad, and clung stubbornly between his fingers. Movement to his right validated his fears. Large shapes appeared at the far side of the field: cows.

"Oh, shit!" he groaned, shaking his hand in an attempt to relieve it of the vile coating. A line of excrement slapped across his cheek. "For fuck's sake!" He shivered, wiped his hand cautiously on the grass, did his best to clean his face, then continued to the next stile, carefully dodging the black circles. He heard a car start up and race off. It faded quickly, leaving him once more in the solitary silence of nature.

He passed the final obstacle and dropped down behind a tall, neatly trimmed hedge. There was no mansion or stately home hidden within the enclosure, only a small bungalow that looked as though it had been transported from a 1950's suburban cul-de-sac. Devoid of light, it looked abandoned amidst the long, wet grass. *Is this it?* he wondered. *Or have I taken the wrong path?* An outside light burst into life, casting his shadow across the stile and into the field beyond. Kurt blinked rapidly and raised a hand to shield his eyes. Somewhere to his right, a door opened, and a pleasant, female voice called out, "Is that you, Kurt?"

"Yes," he replied. *This is it,* he thought, heading to the far side of the property. The windows remained dark, their curtains closed.

"Hurry up, it's freezing!" She was well-spoken, the product of an affluent Home Counties upbringing, he guessed.

Flattening the lapels back over his suit, he went to sweep a hand through his hair, thought better of it, and instead, knelt down and wiped it again on the long, damp grass. He hurried on. The sight of an attractive woman, with curly blonde hair cut to her shoulders, eased the aching and unspoken suspicion that he'd been set up. "Sorry," he said, and smiled. "Miss Zharkova?"

"No, I'm Emma. Come in." She returned his smile and stepped aside, holding the door open for him.

"I'm afraid I'm a bit messy."

"That's fine," she said. "It's cold, hurry up. Come on in."

This is it, Kurt thought, pleased to be welcomed by such a pleasant and beautiful lady. *Am I treading in your footsteps, Tanya? Will I find out what happened to you? Or even find you here, held against your will?*

I'll hold you tight and tell you how much I love you. How much I missed you. How much I need you. How sorry I am...

He entered the property.

Chapter Three

Emma double-locked the door, slipped the bottom bolt across, and asked Kurt to do the same with the one at the top. He obliged, wondering if his potential employer was merely being paranoid or had legitimate reasons to be this cautious. She entered the security code, protecting the sequence and numbers with her torso.

If Tanya's here, maybe they are *keeping her against her will,* he mused. He took a deep breath, enjoying the sweet, fresh scent of Emma's expensive perfume.

Accompanied by three loud beeps, the light on the alarm switched from green to red. "There," she said, turning around to face him. "All done."

"That's quite a security system," he remarked.

"We can't be too careful," Emma replied. "We *are* in the middle of nowhere."

"Yes, I noticed. Are there many problems around here?"

"There's problems everywhere. This way."

Kurt smiled. Emma's casual attire of grey joggers, a pink sweatshirt and fluffy, open toe slippers looked as out-of-place in the mundane bungalow as he felt. He glanced along the hallway, discreetly trying to spot a bathroom.

"Come on," she said. Her layered bob bounced as she walked quickly away. She had a good form—thin at the waist, wide at the hips, with gentle shoulders and an ass that wiggled as she hurried along the corridor. The central line of her G-string was visible beneath her grey joggers.

"Is there somewhere I can clean up?" Kurt asked, staring at the closed doors that lined the drab hallway.

Emma spun around like a ballerina. "Oh, I see." She raised her eyebrows and smiled. "You can leave your shoes in the changing room, the first door on the right, and get them later. There's a sink there too. You'd better be quick though, Katie's waiting."

"Thanks." Kurt disappeared into the small room where he washed his hands and face and checked for any visible marks from the trees; other than a faint trace of red across his forehead, he appeared unscathed. He grabbed some tissue and cleaned his trousers as best he could, then removed his shoes. He considered removing his sodden sock as well, but decided, for the sake of decency, to ring it out and put it back on. He might leave a damp footprint, but that would dry out and hopefully he wouldn't squelch.

He returned to the corridor where Emma was waiting patiently at the far end. "Come on," she said, holding a lift door open. "Katie's waiting."

"Sorry about the footprint," he replied as he checked his feet. "I put my foot in a puddle."

Emma shook her head briefly. "Don't worry, if you stay, cleaning will be one of your duties."

He offered a polite smile.

"That was well concealed," he said, noting how the light switch doubled as a lift call button. "It looks like a bungalow, but I guess it's not."

"The ground floor is," she said, as the doors opened.

He followed Emma inside, stepping to the left while she rested her back on the wall to the right.

"How far down does it go?"

"All the way, of course!" She had a friendly, almost mischievous smile. It was welcome and put him at ease, helping him banish memories of the taxi driver, the black wood and the cowpat, along with any trepidation concerning his impending interview. He

could see how the comforting warmth of someone as friendly and approachable as Emma might easily have been the first lure for Tanya. If she had left him of her own will, that was. Someone pleasant and easy-going. Someone to talk to. Someone that would listen. A woman who could empathise with the all-consuming pain that had taken Tanya to a very dark place...

Above them, the lift wheels whirled rapidly and it began its controlled descent.

"Are you prepared?" Emma asked. "I was terrified when I had my interview, although I didn't have to go through the woods, or do some of the things you'll have to do."

"Miss Zharkova is your employer?"

Emma nodded. "Kind of. More like confidante..." She paused, searching for a more appropriate word. "Lover."

Lover, Kurt thought. *Miss Zharkova's a lesbian? And so is Emma? Or bisexual, at least. Did* they *seduce Tanya? But then why hadn't she told me she was leaving? Because she'd already left mentally and emotionally,* he realised. He knew that was the truth and that it was only a matter of time before she would have left physically, too. Kurt took a deep breath and focused on his game plan. As far as Miss Zharkova was aware, he was simply there as a potential employee.

"Have you been here for very long?" he asked Emma.

"A while."

"Do you like it?"

"It's amazing, though it can be a bit weird." Emma's mischievous smile returned. "She's dark and mysterious."

"Dark and mysterious?"

"Your tie's skew-whiff," she replied, avoiding his question. She stepped closer, clasped the knot in one hand and wiggled the blue cloth into a straight line. "Katie wouldn't be impressed. She likes smart men. Well-presented. Whatever they're wearing... if anything." She returned to the wall. Her back arched, her breasts thrust forward, nipples poking through the pink material of her sweatshirt.

"If anything?"

"You did read the small print?"

Kurt smiled awkwardly. "Scanned."

"Scanned? Someone's in for a surprise. How desperate are you for work?" Emma put a hand to the side of her mouth and whispered, "Don't worry, consider me an ally."

"Work has been quiet. Unfortunately, there aren't many positions available at the moment," he confided. "I signed on to a new agency, hoping for work, and they got me this interview."

"Why's that?"

"What, the agency?"

"No, the positions," she answered.

"According to the agency, a lot of positions are going to the Italians. Apparently, they provide excellent service."

"Hot Latin blood," Emma said, and smiled.

Kurt smiled back. Despite his intentions, she made him feel at ease.

"Don't worry," Emma said, "you'll be perfect for Katie. She loves desperate boys. Personally, I think you'll fit in just fine." The lift pinged, and the doors swiftly opened.

Kurt raised his eyebrows at the broad, carpeted hallway, with niches staggered equidistant on either side. A soft, amber light warmed into life, highlighting the nearest statue. Life-size, it was a perfect imitation of a pot-bellied woman with large breasts, draped in a thick animal skin and carved from grey stone.

"Come on," Emma said, stepping past him.

Hopeful that his damp sock didn't leave too much of a mark, he followed. There was a sweet fragrance to the warm hallway. It alleviated what might have been stale air, replacing it with a pleasant hint of orange and pine.

Despite her cheerful smile, the narrow eyes of the statue were cold. A pair of over-extended incisors descended from a band of gleaming teeth to hang down from her smiling mouth. *Weird,* Kurt thought. *Is this what Emma meant, that Miss Zharkova has an eclectic taste in art?* It reminded him of a prehistoric goddess.

As they approached, a yellow light sprang to life, illuminating the next statue. It was on the opposite side and featured a naked man kneeling. He was muscular, with hands at his sides and head bowed. Heavy balls hung below a rigid phallus that jutted almost vertically between his legs.

"I see Miss Zharkova enjoys her art," he commented.

"In stone and in life," Emma replied, stopping at the first door on the left. "Your instructions are in here. Read them, make your decision, and come back out. I will know what choice you have made when you return. We shall either continue with your interview, or I will show you the way out."

"Thank you," Kurt said. He turned the handle and stepped inside.

The room was compact and comfortable, with two armchairs on the left and a small, circular table on the far side. An open chest, empty, was set to the right of the door. Placed in the centre of the table was an envelope with his name written in swirling calligraphic arcs. An elaborate mural of dancers cavorted around the walls, reminding Kurt of a Witches' Sabbath. In place of the goat god, a blonde woman was seated before the decadent attendants. Her smile and gaze was crafted to fall upon Kurt as he slipped carefully into the nearest chair. He opened the envelope and read. Then reread. He turned it over to check the back. It was blank. He checked inside the envelope, then reread the letter again, slower this time, in case he'd misread a word, or misunderstood a sentence.

His heart raced at the request. He read the letter again. There were only two sentences. The first sentence contained words that sunk to his stomach, made his heart beat faster, and yet, unexpectedly, brought a heat to his groin:

If you wish to proceed, you must remove your clothes, <u>everything</u>. Place them in the chest, lock it, then return to the hallway.

The second line offered an immediate ultimatum:

If you do not wish to proceed or are unable to complete this request, then you must leave now.

He stared up at the mural. A dark-haired woman, robed in a classical gown, danced towards her seated queen. Her infectious smile reminded him of Emma and he let out a solitary laugh. This was definitely the strangest interview he'd ever experienced. He'd met and worked for some eccentrics before, but this woman, whoever she was—and despite his arduous attempts at research, he had discovered nothing about her—was in a class of her own. Surely this was a joke. A YouTuber setting him up. A TV show recording his reaction.

Questions blazed through his mind. Maybe she did know why he was really there and this was their way of getting rid of him. That was one theory, but there was a far more plausible explanation: Miss Zharkova was simply checking for bugs, hidden mics, cameras, that kind of thing. Perhaps she had been secretly recorded before and blackmailed because of it. But then why didn't they scan him before he got in the taxi or at the front door? Wasn't that the usual way to check for bugs? Their request was something else. A test perhaps? Why hadn't they offered him alternative clothing? A boiler suit, or at least let him retain his underwear. Maybe there were clothes waiting for him in the next room. He reread the letter one last time, took a deep breath, and knew that if he was going to find out if Miss Zharkova was involved in Tanya's disappearance, then he had to proceed.

Kurt was proud of his body. It was strong and well-formed, though he secretly wished his average-sized penis was a couple of inches longer. But he had a firm, well-rounded backside that Tanya had liked and that regularly received compliments, along with strong, broad shoulders.

He stripped quickly and efficiently, pleased to finally be rid of his damp sock, but nevertheless nervous at what might happen next. He folded everything neatly, placed the items in the chest, closed it, took a calming breath, and locked it. He gave himself a once-over, rubbed his penis in the hope of bringing it to life and impressing Emma, then took a deep breath, asked himself, *what the hell am I doing?* and stepped out.

Emma's face brightened into a huge grin as her gaze ran over his nude form. "You're staying! Good! Come on."

"Naked?" he queried, following her along the hallway. The carpet felt bouncier without his socks, its thick woollen pile brushing against his skin. He opted to keep his eyes straight ahead. The last thing he needed now was an unwanted erection. Emma's perfume smelt good, sweet and flowery, like a bath of summer roses.

The next statue was female. Dressed in a classical Greek gown, she resembled the lead dancer from the Witches' Sabbath. There was no infectious smile with this lady. Instead, her striking pose, with arms raised and one foot stepped in front of the other, felt threatening. "I understand why Miss Zharkova might take such precautions," he said, "but isn't there something I can wear temporarily?"

"You'll be alright." Emma glanced back, and down, a twinkle in her eyes.

Kurt felt his desire rise.

The next statue, on the left, was male. He, too, was standing, and sported a bold erection. He looked Scandinavian, painted with blond hair and icy-blue eyes.

Emma came to a halt in front of a wooden door on the right. "We're here." The door boasted the image of a nude male kneeling before a semi-clothed lady. She sat on a raised throne, her wide smile offering two fangs as she leant forward, breasts exposed, legs hidden beneath a long skirt. "Katie's in here." Emma stepped to the side. "Good luck. I hope you pass."

"Thanks," he said.

"You've got a perfect bum. You'll fit in well."

Kurt grinned awkwardly. He was far more self-conscious and nervous than he wanted to admit. His heart thumped hard and his penis seemed to have shrunk into his body. He reached for the handle, hesitated, and glanced at Emma.

She smiled. "Go on," she urged. "Katie won't bite... unless she doesn't like you. That's a lie, actually. She'll bite if she likes you as well."

Emma's comments didn't help. Kurt took another deep breath, turned the handle and stepped cautiously into the room. He stopped immediately. The door slammed shut behind him. He heard a lock turn, then nothing. The room was black. Pitch black. Blacker than the woods where the trees had closed in on him. This was an utter darkness that tore into him and stole his inner light, leaving him chilled, not to the bone, but to the depths of his soul.

"Is this a joke?" His words hung heavy in the air before him, as though even the gaseous molecules had been weighted by the darkness. "Hello?"

No sound answered his blunt greeting. He opted to try the door again, half turned, then stopped. Something moved. He was certain of it. Despite the absence of heat, beads of sweat clung to his hands. He rubbed his fingers against his palms and listened. His breath sounded tight and laboured, as though it too were afraid of being snatched up by the unseen force before him, behind him, all around him. He strained to listen. *Yes, it's there, over to the left.* It sounded like... the brush of clothes? The grinding of teeth?

"Hello?" he said again. His words sounded muffled, as though a hand had been placed over his mouth, stifling his speech. He stepped forward, arms outstretched in imitation of his journey through the woods, only this time, he just wanted to leave. To get out. Run away. He retreated and checked the door. It was locked. *Is this what happened to you, Tanya? Trapped in an underground bunker from which you couldn't escape? God, what is this?*

He spun around and listened again. Nothing. Cautiously, he moved further into the room. It was like playing a deadly version of blind man's buff, one where he was naked and vulnerable and terrified of catching the other, whoever that might be. He cut his movement completely as something swept past him. It was fast and cold and spiralled about him, stealing the remnants of warmth from his body before it was lost to the blackness.

Kurt shivered and backed slowly away. His stomach muscles clenched across his belly as though solidifying into plated armour. His penis retreated like a mouse into its home. *This isn't normal.* He wanted to return to Emma. To see her warm smile and enjoy that beautiful perfume. Yet she had locked him in. *Unless...*

Was Emma part of some sinister game? Was she the friendly face to a monstrous organisation? People traffickers, serial killers, snuff film makers... He didn't like the place his thoughts were taking him. He cut them off in favour of Tanya's name. It reverberated through his mind, becoming a mantra that would lead him to safety. He gritted his teeth and attempted to retrace his steps. *I won't go down without a fight. I'll fight my way out and find you, Tanya. We'll escape together and I'll return with the police.*

If he was right, the door was somewhere behind him, somewhere through the shroud of darkness, the darkness that was, in some indefinable way, driving into his mind and body, clouding his senses, dragging him downwards like a resurrected corpse drags the living into its grave.

"Hello, Kurt," a soft voice said as he felt himself collapse beneath the mass of black. "Welcome."

Chapter Four

Kurt struggled to breathe. The air condensed around him, its nebulous quality congealing like viscous oil dragged from the second circle of hell. His legs went rigid as though impaled by steel rods. His arms hung tight at his sides. Any thoughts of self-preservation were supplanted by an impulsive yet overwhelming urge: he didn't want to shield himself from this strange presence. He wanted to know it, feel it, experience it. Whatever it was, there was a powerfully erotic lure like a siren's song that banished all thought of anything else; of Tanya and Emma and the world outside as it beckoned him to know what lay behind the darkness.

The woman's voice returned, soothing him through the impenetrable black. "Will you serve me, Kurt, with your mind, body and soul?"

Her words hung in the air as though strung before him like blossom floating on the wind. He clung to them desperately; a drowning man grasping for a lifeline. *Will you serve me, Kurt, with your mind, body and soul?* Every syllable teased an intimate desire. He heard his answer rather than spoke it, as though he were a witness to the unfolding events. "Yes." *Wait. What? What am I saying?*

The darkness responded before he could retract his words, banishing any superstitious fears as it solidified around him. A smooth hand caressed his backside. Long fingernails scratched superficial lines that provoked unseen hairs to stand on end. He tensed as her fingers slid across the base of his spine, skirting over his hip to rest upon his thigh. He shuddered. His cock twitched but remained limp.

A warning sensation swept up from the depths of his mind, urging him to protect himself against the embrace of the gnawing darkness, reminding him that he was here for Tanya. He pushed it away. He wanted more of her. More words whispered like a song on a summer's breeze. More of her intoxicating touch floating over his naked flesh. More knowledge of who this strange creature was. He wanted her.

He sensed her behind him, still lost in the darkness. A hand cupped his balls, the other clasped his member. Her chin rested on his shoulder. He gasped and made to face her.

"No," she breathed, stroking him slowly to life. Her hands were hot like flesh warmed before a ravenous fire. Her breasts pressed against the frame of his back. He felt her move against him, writhing as her hand slid back and forth over his hardening shaft. Her words whispered delights to accompany the enticing sensations. "Will you protect me, Kurt? Serve me? Fulfil my desires? Obey my wishes and accept my commands?" She squeezed his cock as though affirming her authority over him.

"I will," he replied, despite himself. *Tanya,* he thought, feeling like Peter thrice denying Christ. He shuddered and tried to turn again. Her arms locked against him, bracketing his body in place as her hard nipples massaged a figure of eight against him. Gradually her strokes increased, rising to a healthy rhythm. She kept her movements deliberate, not fast enough to bring the release he desired, nor slow enough to be tortuous. Rather, each steady stroke overrode his thoughts of Tanya, pushing them out of his mind while increasing his desire for the unseen presence that dominated his body. Her fingers nurtured and massaged his balls, prompting and tempting, stimulating and arousing.

Her other hand worked over his shaft, teasing his foreskin back to expose the engorged head. He wanted to thrust against this strange woman; pick her up and impale her on his rigid cock. Her hand drove in the opposite direction, trailing the fleshy membrane back over his tip.

He grunted. It was deep and guttural and desperately urgent. "I want to serve you," he gasped, finally spinning around to face her. Frustrating his satisfaction, her form faded into the obsidian cloud.

Kurt staggered forward, blindly worming his way through the unseen room.

When she spoke again, her words were firm yet dissonant, as though multiple voices echoed the same proposition. "I need someone I can rely on. A man who will serve me without question. Who will be loyal. Without commitment to anyone else. Who will protect me from those that wish to harm me."

Commitment, Kurt thought. The forlorn image of Tanya, heart-broken and tear stricken flashed before him. It was gone before he had chance to set his mind aright.

Her words were whispered again, as though she were discarding her lingerie in a trail for him to follow. "Will you look after me, Kurt? Protect me? Satisfy me?"

He spun around, still hopeful of catching her. Hopeful that her intimate attentions might return. He was met by a thick blanket of darkness. "Where are you?"

"I require a man who can be ruthless."

"Ruthless? Where are you?"

"I require a man that will accept me as his queen."

"'His queen'? What's going on? Where are you?" He swung to the right, arms pointed outwards in imitation of his hard cock, and took a few steps. Nothing. He paused, turned to the left and moved again. Only the absorbing darkness greeted him.

When she spoke again, it felt as though her words wrapped around him. There was no focal point to the sound; no direction to turn, no singular being that spoke. "I want a man who will surrender himself to me. Mind and heart, body and blood, sex and soul."

Surrender? Kurt's mind returned Tanya to him. He pictured her, seated habitually in the old, brown leather armchair, cushions clutched tightly in her arms, staring vacantly out of the bay window, barely noticing the world as it streamed past. He hated her for not being stronger, for fading from life into that all-consuming depression. Hated himself for not understanding, for being too scared to talk. Their home had become a gravestone, a bleak marker to the dreams of a happy family.

"I want you, Kurt," Katie said, dissipating the memories of his life with Tanya, "but do you want me? Will you give yourself to me? Help me live a full life?"

"What's going on? Have I been drugged?"

"No, no drugs." Her laconic reply burst forth from the ebony veil directly before him. He jolted back, body poised in self-defence. His rigid penis contrasted his mind's attempt at dispassionate clarity.

Gradually, streaks of amber peeked through the inky blackness, forming into soft oval lights that filtered away the cloud of darkness. Walls solidified behind them, forming a large, empty room. The door was to his right, and to his left three steps led up to a raised platform, carpeted in rose red.

His gaze fell upon the dark-haired beauty, wearing a tight dress cut to the thigh, and seated upon an elegant wooden throne, its high back reminiscent of a pointed collar. Her smooth legs were parted, exposing the black fabric that covered her crotch. Curled over the arms of her elegant seat, long fingernails gleamed an intoxicating red.

Her penetrating stare pressed through the defences of his ego, cutting into the core of his being. He gasped as though she had reached out, clasped his manhood and forced him to orgasm. His gaze dropped to the floor. His hard cock trembled before him, a dribble of pre-cum seeping from its tip. When he looked up, she was still and lifeless; a frozen image, like the sculptured icons in the hallway.

Finally, she smiled. It was a pleasant smile but for the two sharp points that hung ominously behind her upper lip. "Hello, Kurt."

The sight of her fangs confused him. *Was this an act, a well-choreographed play of light and dark, of a temperature controlled room, make-up and special effects?*

He glanced again at the seductive brunette seated calmly upon the stepped platform. He felt vulnerable before her, exposed and yet eager, almost desperate for her attention. He cleared his throat and spoke. "Miss Zharkova?"

"I am."

"Hello," he said. It felt inadequate, a bland greeting that failed to convey the mixture of his true feelings.

Her right hand rose. The polished red of her fingernails reflected the soft light from the surrounding walls as she waved him nearer. "Come closer."

Kurt approached cautiously. Each step affirmed his desire to be near her, countered by a gnawing uncertainty and a growing suspicion that this was no ordinary woman. He stopped at the foot of the platform. His hands rested over his groin, protecting his vulnerability, concealing his arousal.

"Remove your hands."

"Why am I naked?"

"Questions later. You are a handsome young man. Now, remove your hands."

He swallowed, hesitated, then let his hands rest at his sides. His penis remained erect.

Her gaze dropped to his groin. "Why do you wish to serve me?"

"I am a butler by career. The agency told me you needed someone."

"No, there is more, why do *you* wish to serve me?"

"I was intrigued..." He didn't mention his suspicion that she had something to do with the disappearance of his fiancée.

When she didn't answer, he added, "Why was I required to strip?"

Her thumb and fingers brushed her pale chin as she contemplated his answer. "And now? Do you still wish to serve me?"

He wanted to ask her outright; what happened at that party? What did you do to my fiancée? Where is she? The questions teetered on the tip of his tongue. *No,* he thought. *Don't say anything or you might put*

her in danger. Bide your time. Play it safe. Wait for the right moment.
Instead, he replied, "I... I don't know..."
"You don't know?"
"I mean, I don't know what just happened. I... I... I just know that I don't want to leave."
"Then tell me, will you accept everything I ask? Everything?"
His response was spontaneous, reached and concluded before his mind recognised its implications. "Yes."
"I expect to be called Miss."
"Understood, Miss."
"There are conditions you have to meet if I am to accept you as my server."
"Server, Miss Zharkova?"
"Just 'Miss'."
"A server, Miss?"
"The conditions to your employment go far beyond every position you have previously held."
"I understand. Miss."
"In the early days, it will be very difficult for you, but if you accept my guidance, you will receive many benefits, including a long and healthy life."
"Difficult?"
"Will you dedicate your life to me? Serve me without hesitation? Do as I command?"
His answer shot forth, unrestricted by doubt or question. "Yes."
Katie's hand dropped to her thigh, gently stroking the soft flesh. "Kneel, boy."
Obediently, he fell to one knee. His head inclined towards the floor, his cock still vigorously upright.
"Both knees."
He readjusted and looked up at her.

"Masturbate for me. And as you do, I want to hear you tell me why you wish to serve me. Why should I chose you above any other?"

He frowned, then half-smiled in embarrassment and shook his head. "I'm sorry, Miss Zharkova, you want me to do what?"

"I do not like repeating myself, Kurt. You heard me. Wank for me. Now."

His face flushed red. His hand remained limply at his side.

"Do it now, or leave."

His hand felt sluggish, as though he were lifting heavy chains. His fingers wrapped around his member. It was hot and hard, and he began to stroke.

Katie leant forward, her hands on her parted legs. "Look at me. Look into my eyes. Now tell me, why do you wish to serve me?"

Obediently, Kurt stared into the deep pools of seductive brown. Like scrying mirrors, they surfaced hidden appetites that lay dormant beneath a façade of etiquette and civility. Fantasies and memories surged through him, laid bare by the exposure of this most intimate and private of acts. Tanya was there, smiling as she watched him. She was happy and light, alleviated from the heavy darkness that had enveloped everything since it had happened. He pushed her away, remembering how he had come to hate how she was, how he didn't want to be pulled down into that darkness. He focused on the mesmerising woman in front of him. When they came, his words were breathy yet deep, full of desperation and laced with arousal. "Oh my god."

"Goddess," Katie corrected. "Tell me."

"I wish to work for you, to help you..." His brow tightened and he bit his lip. "To achieve your objectives. I wish... to support you... in any way that I am able..."

"Is that all?"

"I am discreet... and can..." His words faded as his hand moved rapidly over his cock. "This is hard," he gasped.

Unimpressed, Katie sat back in her throne. "Tell me."

His words became scattered, broken by his increasing arousal. "Serve you... as you wish. I just... need... to... oh god..."

"Goddess."

"Goddess..."

"More," Katie instructed. "Faster."

"I can't speak," he groaned. His hand answered her command, working tirelessly along his swollen member. Fantasies blanketed his mind. Every urge he possessed, she satiated. Every fear, she allayed. Everything he could be, she revealed as he knelt before her. His hand blasted over his hard cock, fuelling new sensations that swarmed into his consciousness.

Her hand slapped the arm of her throne, creating a dull, lifeless thump. "I said, faster!" She raised her voice, shouting the command. "FASTER! FASTER!"

Kurt gritted his teeth and grunted as he tugged himself violently.

"Good boy," Katie said, closing her eyes. Her face remained pale but for her glossy red lips and the soft trace of dark eye shadow.

Kurt felt like he was floating, soaring above the room. Images of Katie, lying naked beneath him, rushed through his mind. Her legs were spread, her arms outstretched, encouraging him to take her. He blinked, and the image changed. He was seated on her throne, his phallus jutting hungrily upwards. She kissed him, hard and urgent, then planted herself on his lap, sliding down onto his cock. Her hands rested on his shoulders, her breasts plump and rounded before him.

"Accept me as your goddess," she whispered. "I am your princess and your queen. I am the witch that owns your soul. I am the keyholder of your manhood. I am the mistress of your blood." She kissed him again, tenderly this time, as if searching for the perfect caress, then harder, her mouth sliding over his as she rose and fell on his member.

He grunted and clasped her tightly. His fingers clawed over her back, squeezing her ass. His mouth dove hungrily to her breasts, tongue flicking rapidly over her hard nipples. His lips cupped and pulled, then released.

"Good boy," she encouraged.

Her words broke the mirage. Kurt was on the floor again, still kneeling, still wanking. His balls were drawn tight. His hand swiftly pulled himself towards release. He wiped his brow, fingers kneading his forehead as he tried to clear the fog of erotic images. "I'm gonna cum," he moaned.

"Keep going." Katie watched him with interest, her tongue sweeping over her fangs in long, teasing flicks.

Kurt roared as hot streams of cum spurted onto the floor. His hand didn't stop, drawing every last drop from his spasming balls.

A haze of movement streaked before him, lines that muddied human contours as Katie shot behind him. Her hands came to rest upon his shoulders. She was cool, neither warm nor cold, but tepid like the dawn of a summer's day, intimating its impending heat. Her lips brushed his ear as she whispered her satisfaction. "That was a lot."

Before he could respond, her teeth plunged into his neck, breaking through the skin and releasing his red nectar into her mouth. Her arms wrapped around him, pulling him against her as her tongue encouraged the warm blood from his body.

He felt dizzy and disoriented. His vision faded to grey, before twisting and distorting. The throne and steps broke apart and merged into a singularity. He heard her slurping, drawing his blood from his neck. It felt hot, fiery, and yet kindled a need to surrender to the being feeding upon him.

When she released him, he collapsed onto all fours, his cock still twitching from the intense orgasm. He felt weak and wanted to lie down and sleep. A tiny question returned: *What did you do to Tanya?*

"Emma," Katie called. She had returned to her seat where she sat, elegant and majestic in her short dress, cheeks glowing, thighs flushed pink.

Kurt heard the door open then close behind him. It was followed by the comforting flip flop of Emma's slippers. They came to a halt behind his shaking body.

"I am happy for Kurt to join us."

"Brilliant!" Emma exclaimed.

Kurt's gaze was lost on the islands of semen and droplets of blood that patched the polished wooden boards like liquid fire and ice.

"Make sure he is given a cage."

"It's ready for him. I'll tell the driver to go."

"Good," Katie said. "Get up, Kurt."

Unaided, he struggled to his feet.

"I accept you as my server. Emma will see to it that all documents are completed. From this point on, you are mine. You will remain naked unless we go out. Do you understand?"

Kurt felt the ultimatum sink deep to his belly, to the cave the ogre had occupied. If he left, he would never comprehend who or what she truly was. Nor would he ever know if she had lured Tanya from their happy life. *Happy life.* The words haunted him. There were cracks in that happiness. Cracks like a vase that had been shattered and badly glued together again.

"Do you understand, Kurt?" Katie asked.

"I do," he said. He knew then, standing naked and empty before her, that there was no going back. He was hers; completely, totally, and utterly hers. Tanya had gone, along with their future, he would try and find her and take her home, but deep down part of him, a part that he had dared not verbalise before, already sensed that it was too late.

Katie was another world. A world of which he had no understanding, no comprehension of what she was or what had really happened, yet she offered him an exit from his old existence. He was now Katie's and he reckoned, perhaps, in some tiny way, she was also his. At least he wanted her to be.

Chapter Five

"I'm glad you're staying," Emma said, removing the wings of a plaster before she placed it over Kurt's neck. "I thought you might."

"You did?" he enquired, secretly enjoying the close contact.

"Yeah," she said, tapping it gently.

The plaster, coupled with her flowery scent, grounded him in reality. Reaffirmed the realness of the world. It made him wonder if he'd really undergone such an intimate and soul-baring experience. There had been a catharsis to his performance, a naked assertion that at the core of his masculinity there was a display of sexual prowess.

On a deeper level, Katie had broken the metaphorical vase that contained his hopes at finding Tanya and their shared future. Instead, the creature that he had pledged his allegiance to had forced him to listen to that tiny, niggling voice that questioned if there was anything left of his relationship he might save.

"She wants me to stay naked," he stated, feeling a mixture of embarrassment and arousal.

"That's alright. You've got a good body," Emma said, screwing up the wrapper and plastic edges and shoving them in her pocket. "Come on."

"I don't know if I can," he confessed, watching her walk off along the statue corridor.

Emma stopped beside the statue of the bold Viking. "You agreed."

"Why naked?"

"It gets better," Emma advised, a twinkle in her eyes.

"Better? How?" Kurt asked, aware that she was teasing.

"Geez, for a fit young guy, you're so naïve."

"I'm not into the fetish scene," he said.

"You think this is a fetish?" Emma asked. She walked off. Kurt glanced at the door to the room that had changed his world.

"Isn't it?"

"It's a lifestyle. A very ancient, very special, very..." She paused, searching for the right word before settling on, "blessed lifestyle."
"Blessed?"
"What did Katie tell you?"
"I don't know...that I'd dedicate my life to her."
"Was that it?"
"She said something about being a witch and a mistress of blood."
"And you accepted?"
Emma's words left him feeling nervous. "Yeah," he agreed.
"You needed that."
"Needed what?"
Emma grinned. "You were all pent up. I bet you feel a lot better now."
"I feel tired," he said.
"Come on, I'll take you to your room. You can shower there."
"Wait." He looked at her deep and hard; serious. "I need to know..."
"Know what?"
"Is she, an actress?"
A tinge of humour warmed Emma's face. "An actress?"
Kurt nodded.
She pursed her lips as if mulling over the most appropriate answer. "No, she's not."
"Then what was that? How did she do that? The light, the cold, the visions..."
"You are now part of something that the majority of people will never, ever, *ever* experience, Kurt."
He shook his head, still not able to commit to the realisation that he had experienced something far beyond his world compass. "Which means?"
"Come on," she said.
"No, tell me."

"Kurt, you've been through a very intense experience. You need time to adjust."

"Emma, what is she?"

The blonde stopped and faced him. "Katie doesn't age. She, like they say in the movies, doesn't get old and will never die. She feeds on blood and energy. She is a vampire. A real, no lies, no tricks or special effects, vampire."

He stared at her in disbelief. His mouth partially open.

"Come on," she urged, and continued along the hallway. When he didn't follow she stopped and looked back at him. "I've told you the truth. You just have to accept it." She refused to say any more and Kurt returned with her to the lift in silence. She selected a lower floor. The doors closed and the steel box descended. "After you shower, make sure you put on your cage."

"My cage?"

"Your cock cage," Emma said bluntly.

"My what?"

"Your cock cage. I know you heard Katie, I was there when she mentioned it."

"A cock cage?"

"Yeah, it goes on your willy," Emma said, running her eyes over his limp member.

"What the hell do I need that for?"

"It's to stop you playing with yourself; wanking, or fucking, getting a blowjob."

Kurt's heart thumped a little harder as he visualised Emma kneeling before him. Her small mouth open, her eyes on his as her tongue stretched out to take him.

"I'd try not to think about it," she said, raising an eyebrow at the sight of his twitching cock. Her words washed the image away, leaving the dawn of a bleak reality. She offered a sympathetic smile. "All the servers wear them. It's expected. Well, nearly all and nearly always."

"I don't think I want to do that."

"You agreed. Silly boy. I told you to read the small print."

"No one reads the small print and it probably doesn't talk about things like that. Besides, I haven't signed anything."

"Too late," Emma said. "Anyway, I bought you a nice one. What's your favourite colour?"

"My favourite colour?" Kurt repeated.

"Mhm."

"Blue. Sky blue."

A broad grin burst onto Emma's face. "Good, that's the colour I bought."

"*You* bought it?"

Emma nodded. The lift pinged and the doors opened, this time offering an even longer corridor. Like a domino of magical candles, soft wall lights bloomed into life.

"After you," Kurt said, motioning with his hand.

"Such a gentleman," Emma observed and stepped out into the warm tunnel.

"How far down are we?" he asked, imagining Tanya walking the same corridors.

Emma shrugged. "Oh, I don't know, fifty metres, maybe? It's an old Cold War bunker. Katie had someone buy it for her."

"Someone *bought* it for her?"

"She has lots of benefactors." She put a hand over the side of her mouth and whispered rather loudly, "Money slaves, really. Some are very wealthy."

"Impressive," Kurt commented.

"Your room is here," Emma said, stepping aside and letting Kurt open a functional grey door. Aside from the paint job it looked original.

Another light came on. "Wow," he commented. Panoramic scenes of mountains and woodland lakes bled into one another, enlivening the four walls to create a healthy sense of space and an uncanny experience of natural light. "It's big."

"It was a dormitory for soldiers. I think it contained about twenty beds." Emma stepped in behind him. "Katie had it converted. You've got an en-suite through there." She pointed to an internal door on the forest wall. "And your bedroom's through there." She pointed to another one, also on the same wall and set between the trunks of two realistically-painted yew trees.

"Nice, thank you," he said. "You want me to move in now?"

"Yes, they should have told you that," Emma advised.

"They did. I just hoped that I could go home and collect my things, or we'd arrange a date, that kind of stuff."

"Sorry, Kurt."

"I was really hoping you might just give me a day."

"You've got everything you need already," Emma said, "and besides, you're here now. Your things can be collected later."

"I guess so." He stared at the ceiling painting. An elevated blue sky fed the four images into a perfect unity while simultaneously alleviating the closeting oppression from the earth above.

"And that's for you," Emma said, pointing to a small box on the table nearest to the door.

"What is it?" Kurt asked, already knowing the answer. He eyed it cautiously as if it belonged to Pandora.

Emma nodded, her face serious. "If I were you, I'd go shower. Freshen up and then put it on. I'll help you, if you like."

"Help me?"

"I've seen them on lots of men."

"Er..." Kurt looked confused. "What about women?" he queried, wondering if Tanya had been amongst the numerous people that Emma had seen pass through the underground bunker.

"They're not in chastity if that's what you mean. Not usually."

"What happens to them?"

"What, the women?"

"Yes."

"They come, they go. They're not locked up in a sex dungeon if that's what you're asking."

"Good," he said, "I mean, are they kept naked as well?"

"No, not usually, that's just for you men. Chastity, too."

"Where do they all go?" he asked. "The men and women?"

"Most go back to their lives. They serve her when she requires, and some, like myself, may live with her."

"Nowhere else?"

"She doesn't keep a track of everyone," Emma said.

"I just wondered." He smiled, pleased that the possibility of Tanya's presence was solidifying into something more than a vague hope. His fingers ran over the plaster that covered his neck wound. The only evidence beyond his memories and empty balls that his experience with Katie had been tangible.

"Go shower, I'll come back in fifteen minutes. Is that long enough?"

"Er, yes, okay."

"Good. I'll see you soon."

*

Kurt was fresh from the shower when Emma returned. A towel was wrapped around his waist, covering his groin but exposing the firm bundle of muscles across his abdomen. A snatch of hair trailed beneath the green fibres of his thick towel.

"The towel's got to go," she said, noting the box lid was now open. The table remained absent of its contents.

"It's just a towel," he stated.

"Naked," Emma asserted. "You dry yourself with a towel, you don't wear it."

"I don't see what the problem is."

"Did you put it on?"

"No, I looked at it, that's all."

"Right, lose the towel." She grabbed the box and turned it upside down. The contents clattered onto the table. She organised them into a row of items, then turned to face him.

"You aren't serious?" he asked, shaking his head as he studied its contents. There were only a few items: a few small, plastic pins of varying lengths, one of which appeared like an oversized needle with an eye at its tip, a sequence of half circles, a thicker arced piece of plastic with two plastic bars that pointed out in parallel lines on either side, and a blue tube shaped like a limp penis.

"You don't want to annoy her," she warned, and picked up an incomplete plastic ring.

"How long is this for?"

"You'll have to ask Katie." Emma handed Kurt the item and selected another identical piece of plastic. "I told you to lose the towel."

Hesitantly, he removed the makeshift garment, throwing it over the back of the sofa.

"Good," Emma said and passed Kurt the second piece. "Put them together..." She paused as Kurt scissored the two halves into a circle. "Then put them behind your shaft and balls, so your balls are in front."

"Emma," he said, looking down at himself. "I don't think I can do this."

Her face stiffened. "You don't want to go down that road."

"I can leave, can't I?" he countered.

"You've already agreed." When he didn't answer, she added, "Besides, what have you got to go back to?"

"My life."

"Your life? What life? She knows a lot more about you than you realise."

"What do you mean?"

"Like most employers, she checks on the people she employs."

Kurt hesitated, wondering to what extent Katie knew he was looking for Tanya. "And you," he replied, redirecting his thoughts, "were you checked?"

"I was vetted. Just like you."

"Just like me?"

"Yes," Emma confirmed, "just like you. Now, stop being so silly and put it on. Or, I'll do it for you."

He looked down at himself again. His balls hung loose and heavy. His neatly shaven cock was flaccid but not so small as to be embarrassing. With Emma's attention, he felt as though it could easily rise to erection.

"Lift your balls and slip it around the back," Emma instructed, remaining clinically professional.

Kurt eased the open plastic band around himself, then pushed the two sides together to form a ring where a hole lined up in the top centre of the plastic.

"Good," Emma said, holding up what looked like a blunt plastic needle. "Push this through the hole. That'll lock these in place."

Again, Kurt followed her command. He sealed the two sides together by adding the needle that slotted into the small hole and jutted out above the length of his dick.

"Now, the sheath." Emma handed him the hard plastic tube. It looked like a long nose with small holes at its tip and on either side. He pushed it over his dick. It retracted his foreskin as he slid it over himself, and he took it off and pulled the loose skin further forward over his helmet and tried again, until the hole at the base of the sheath slipped over the pin.

"Now this one," Emma said, handing Kurt a smaller clasp. "This one goes in front of your balls."

"Are you serious?"

"You don't want to know what happened to her last server," Emma warned.

"Why?"

Emma shrugged.

"What happened?"

"He didn't listen."

That doesn't sound good. "That sounds like a threat."

"A warning," Emma suggested. "You are now the server to Katie Zharkova: Keyholder, entrepreneur, Sister of Annis, vampire."

"Vampire," Kurt repeated, savouring the sound of the word as if he were tasting a fine wine.

"Give it time to sink in and anyway, you're here now. You swore to serve her. There's nothing you can do."

"I could leave."

"Can you? You've said that a couple of times now."

"You could help me."

Emma laughed. "You don't want to leave though, do you," she said, with certainty. "You want to know."

"Know?" *She does know about Tanya.* "What do you mean?"

"You want to know," Emma said. "You want answers. Is this real? Can I really do this? Will I find meaning to my empty life? Can I close the door on my past and start again? Questions so many servers have."

The image of his empty house burst into his mind. It was filled with darkening memories and pangs of conscience. The haunting reminder of Tanya's absence when he returned home from work and sat opposite her empty seat. The seat by the window where she had taken up residence day-in, day-out, barely watching the world as it raced by without her. The vacant side of the bed, absent of her smell, her shape, her heat, her love. The space at the dinner table where he relived his silence as he ignored her desperate need for communication, for acknowledgement, for acceptance of her pain. He imagined talking to her, telling her how he truly felt. How much he felt their loss, too. They would cry and hug and kiss and start afresh. Better, stronger, more understanding and open to one another.

"I..." Kurt's words choked in his throat as he stared at Emma. His mind's eye still at home. The image of their open front door flashed into his mind; a gaping hole like the wound in Tanya's heart. In his heart. Bared to the cutting chill of winter. A real-world representation, just like the empty cot in Lotte's room.

"She has you now, Kurt," Emma said, "and there's not very much that you can do about it."

He stared at the blonde, remembering only Tanya. Tears bound firmly in his eyes as he held her tightly, affirming that no pain would ever touch her again. "I'm so sorry," the doctor had said, and left. *Tanya,* Kurt thought. *Where are you?*

"Kurt," Emma prompted.

He took a deep breath and raised the internal dam against the emotions once more. "Sorry."

"It's okay," she said. "Bad memories?"

"I don't want to talk about it." He shook his head like a dog expunging water from its coat. "I'm fine." He looked down at himself. "Is she going to let me out of this?"

"Kurt, she's going to turn your world inside out."

His exasperated sigh punctuated his decision. He pressed the second clasp in place, bringing the two sides together, enabling the pin to slot through the opening and also lock it in place.

"Padlock." Emma handed him the small metal item.

"Where's my key?" he asked.

"Katie is your keyholder," Emma informed him. "Sometimes, she locks the boys herself, but she is tired and needs to rest."

"Okay, but where's my key?"

"Doubtful."

"Doubtful?" Kurt frowned again. He shook his head. "You want me to lock myself in this without giving me a key or knowing when I will be let out?"

Emma looked serious. "Yes."

"When do I get unlocked?"

"You'll have to ask Katie," Emma replied, avoiding a direct answer. "Close it."

Kurt hesitated. It was small, a tiny padlock by all standards. He took a moment, remembered his goal: *I am here to find Tanya and take her home with me.* He took a deep breath and snapped it shut. *One door closes, another one opens. It better or I'm out of here.*

"There," Emma said happily. "Now you're ready."

"Ready?"

"For your new life. Katie needs you to get the car ready later. First, I'll show you around."

"Okay," he said, checking himself. The cock cage felt weird, like an artificial appendage and slightly uncomfortable. There was also a strangely arousing sense of vulnerability that he hadn't anticipated; he was at their mercy, and being required to remain naked, everyone would know. Imaginary situations of humiliating exposure surged through his mind. Strangers would laugh. They'd see him as ridiculous and impotent; a gullible young man who'd been seduced by a...a...vampire. It felt strange acknowledging it as fact yet when pressed, Emma's answer had been deadly serious. Katie was not the product of elaborate make-up or hi-tech sound and light effects, she was, as clearly as the blood that had trickled down his neck, a vampire.

"Are you okay?" Emma asked.

"This has to be a joke."

Emma shook her head. Her words, spoken with a quiet intensity, underlined her seriousness. "Kurt, none of it is a joke and deep down you know that."

He looked down at himself, at his fleshy body joined by the blue cage that sheathed his dick.

"Come on. There's a world to explore," she said.

"A world?" *What kind of world?* he wondered.

"First, this floor." Emma headed out into the corridor. "Next to and opposite your room there are three rooms for visiting servers."

"Where's your room?"

"Why? Do you want to clean it already?"

"I'm cleaning too?"

She grinned. "I did tell you. Most of the rooms on this floor are utility rooms. At the end of the corridor is the generator room. There is another exit, though it's locked. Katie and I have the access codes. You'll get them if you prove yourself. The other rooms," she said, as they peered down the corridor, "are store rooms. Some are sealed and are solely for Katie. You may be required to clean or retrieve items from the others, if Katie decides to change the décor of a room."

"Okay," Kurt said, intrigued by the idea of Katie's stores. "What's in there?"

"The contents of a life long lived."

"I have access?"

"Eventually," she confirmed, and smiled. "But not yet. Let's go to the next floor." She headed back to the lift.

"This is noisy," he noted, as his padlock clattered against the sheath.

"Think of it like a bell." Emma grinned. "We'll always know where you are."

"Funny," he said, and clasped it in his hand to stifle the noise. They got in and went up a couple of floors.

The doors opened to another long corridor. "This is where you'll spend a lot of your time. Unless Katie is expecting guests, in which case you'll be on the ground floor."

"What floor is this?" Kurt asked.

"This is three; they're all minus because they're underground, but we don't bother with that."

"I'm on five," he stated. "Minus five."

"Good maths. You get a brownie point," she said, leading Kurt through the building.

"I feel like a cow with a cow bell, or a jester," he said.

She grinned. "Just don't start mooing or someone might milk you – though you'd probably like that." He smiled awkwardly and she continued the guided tour, answering some questions, leaving others to hang in the air, while gradually leading him back up to the ground floor. "You'll find your clothes in the garage," she concluded.

"Clothes?"

"You won't always be naked – at home you will – but when you go out, you'll be dressed. We don't need to draw attention to ourselves, and with you being such a cute hottie, you'll be noticed if you're walking around naked."

"I see," he said, doing his best to battle the sinking feeling that he was way out of his depth.

Chapter Six

This was the right place. Katie sensed it. She needed blood—fresh blood, blood purified by sattvic rites—and right now, that blood was pumping through the humans exiting the small, almost insignificant Sangha. Glowing with benevolent energy, the place was like a spiritual beacon amidst the dull vibrations of the surrounding homes. Its energy would help her recover from her transformation into the black cloud. Feeding on Kurt, who was discreetly waiting some distance away in her car, had helped, but she needed an energetic pick-me-up, something that would nourish her being.

She'd chosen a good spot on the opposite side of the road, where she played the role of the impatient girlfriend, constantly checking her phone while waiting for an absent partner.

The semi-detached house looked ordinary for all intents and purposes. The kind of fixer-upper a couple planning a family would quickly snap up were it at the right price. Two first floor windows overlooked the trimmed lawn, centred by a path of slabs that led to the front door, where a statue of a meditating Buddha sat like a poster boy for the contemplative religion. An aura of red light pulsed around it, saturating the door and coating the walls and windows with toxic flames that would burn into Katie if she tried to enter. That didn't bother her. She had other ideas.

She watched Buddhists leave like Lilith perusing the animals as they left the ark. She compared the upstanding to the lame, the fit to the unhealthy, the young and virile to the aged and infertile. She knew which ones would replenish her body and feed her soul and would choose the most suitable to do just that.

The first to leave was an elderly woman, dressed in rainbow-coloured trousers and a thick, blue coat. A deep glow of gnawing red light throbbed about her right side as she limped away from the property. It reminded Katie of an open wound. She let the woman continue unharmed.

A middle-aged man was next. He was tall and fit, and despite a slender face that seemed a little too long, he possessed a calm demeanour whose presence would bring comfort to those around him.

There'll be better, Katie thought.

He paused at the gate to rummage in his pocket for his car keys. The hazard lights of a silver six-seater flashed, accompanied by wing mirrors that opened to their external position. The soft, green light around the centre of his chest conveyed comforting sensations of lying in the long, teasing grass of a summer's field, where fears and worries were unable to intrude. He got into his people carrier, glanced briefly at Katie, and drove off.

Individuals and groups followed, exiting the converted home. Two young women hurried across the road. There was no magnificent aura or sacred halo to indicate any profound spiritual development. Rather, their astral bodies flashed with oranges and blues, darted with traces of yellow and sparks of green. They smelt clean and fresh, the flowery scent of their earlier showers still pleasantly strong.

A subtle yet calming aroma of lavender brought Katie's attention towards the brunette. She was slim and attractive, in her early twenties, Katie estimated, with an adventurous look in her eye that might, on another occasion, have tempted Katie to take her as a pet. Her companion had a dark complexion with a small nose and ears hidden behind long black hair. Her shower gel contained a hint of lemon, diluted amidst a subtle backdrop of cool mint.

Watching them pass, Katie contemplated following. *Double the pleasure,* she thought. She opted to wait, sensing there was a better prize to be had.

Her clairsentience was answered immediately as a young man appeared in the doorway. His auburn hair was shaved neatly from collar to ear and left longer but still smartly cut atop his head. He pulled the collar of his leather jacket up around his neck, called out, "Goodbye," then closed the door behind him and walked purposefully along the path.

Katie honed in on his movement. *This one is rare*, she thought, sensing the arrow of concentration that lay behind his every step. She was familiar with his mindset. There was no sacrifice involved in his focus, no banishment of intrusive sounds or irritating distractions. Rather, it was an inclusive knowing, an observing awareness in which everything was heightened. From the delightful odours of the nearby curry house to the distant bus pulling away into traffic, and beyond that, the passenger plane flying high above. He had tapped into her vampiric reality, and as such, she knew instantly that he was the one. *Perfect. Refined energy. Just what I need.*

He reached the gate, recently painted orange, turned left, and headed down the road. His pace remained slow, almost cautious, as he devoured every detail of his journey. She knew he was aware of her, though it wasn't until he crossed the road that he glanced back. He caught her eye, then disappeared into the catacombs of a housing estate.

As she mirrored his steps, her mind became blank. No thoughts floated into her consciousness, no emotions burst or sparked memories or desires that would flash outwards and betray her presence. Gradually, she was muted from the world as though her being had faded into nothingness. She walked on, unseen, following him until he disappeared into the garden of a detached property.

She turned right and stopped. He was at the door. He turned his key and opened it. Katie rushed past him, shooting like a gust of wind through the gap between body and doorframe, up the stairs and following energetic memories into his bedroom.

She heard the front door close, the chain slip across, followed by his greeting to his parents. "I'm home." He had a pleasant voice. It was calm and relaxing, and under other circumstances might even soothe Katie to sleep. But she wasn't there to sleep.

"Alright, son," a man's deep voice responded.

"Hi, David, how did it go?" his mother asked.

Katie listened to them talk as she moved quietly through his room, surveying the evidence of his few years of life. There were no posters of models on the walls, either female or male, no homage to a band or a film he particularly enjoyed. His room was a shrine to the Lord Buddha and his teachings.

A double bed, neatly made, was placed opposite the bay window. Above its head was an elaborate poster of the Lord Buddha surrounded by colourful bodhisattvas, beautiful gods and fiery demons.

She stopped at the window and flicked through the book of death meditation that waited, bookmark in place, for his return. It was contrasted by a fitness magazine and a stack of sports games that lay beside a games machine. On the eastern wall, a Buddhist shrine was set between two inbuilt wardrobes with candles, statues, incense, and a set of mantra cards waiting to be used. The wardrobe on the right, closest to the desk and window, was closed. Its companion, on the left, was ajar, spewing clothes onto the floor.

Katie slipped into the messy wardrobe. Her body trembled as she pushed past his hanging clothes and into the wall itself. It gave way, as though she were shouldering through a crowd of people. Everything stalled as she waited in the shadows. It felt like being frozen in time, caught between the cracks of the living and the non-existent. She heard him trundle up the stairs, a slow, methodical pace, closer to fatigued movement than a meditative walk.

A sharp slice of yellow cut into the room as the landing light burst into life, bringing clarity to the wardrobe's gloomy contents. The bedroom door opened, imparting brightness as though the Enlightened One were revealing Himself.

David placed a mug of herbal tea on the bedside cabinet, then disappeared into the bathroom. He was back within a few minutes, swapping the overhead light for the bedside lamp. He stripped off to reveal a firm, muscular body with few hairs, and slipped into bed.

He didn't take long to fall asleep, after drinking half his tea and saying a quiet prayer, then killing the light and fading into the comforting blackness.

Caught between the world of form and formlessness, Katie waited, allowing minutes to pass into hours. His parents headed upstairs, chatting quietly, and disappeared into the bathroom, then bedroom. It was not long before the deep snores of his father could be heard alongside the gentle breath of his mother.

Katie stepped forth from her hypnagogic slumber, emerging from the wardrobe to stand beside him.

He was a handsome man, with wide shoulders and good, toned muscles. A gentle glow enveloped his body as he slept. It was light and airy, like a sunny haze penetrating a mist-coated wood.

Yes, she thought, recalling the sour taste Kurt's blood had left in her mouth. *He'll do nicely.*

Like a scavenging raven, Katie perched on the edge of his bed. She pushed off her heels and coat, and slipped in behind him, lifting the duvet to marry her slender form against his bare back. The curve of his buttocks rested between the arch of her pelvis. Comforted by the heat of his body, her hand came to rest against the firm contours of his stomach. He murmured an incoherent affirmation. Katie's other hand stroked his hair, soothing him as she leaned forward and whispered into his ear, "Accept me."

Her left hand descended, fingernails scraping over neatly trimmed pubic hair, then lower, brushing over his member. He responded quickly, hardening at her touch. He was a good size, larger than average, with a pleasing girth.

"What?" he murmured, withdrawing from the depths of sleep. He went to turn around.

Katie's hand pulled on him quickly, providing healthy strokes that forced his attention to her movements.

David gasped and attempted to face her again.

"No," she whispered. Her grip dissolved. Her fingers splayed outwards, dancing teasingly as they descended where fingernails scraped the gravelly skin of his ball sack.

"Who are you?" he groaned.

"Accept me," she whispered, and kissed his neck. "Close your eyes." Her fingers clasped him again. She squeezed then stroked. "Close your eyes." Her lips vibrated against the firm flesh of his neck.

He groaned again. It was a deep, resonating grunt. "Who are you?"

"Just relax, David," she whispered. "Just relax."

Her hand replaced her words, speaking through friction and pressure. Guiding and manipulating. "You are so relaxed," she continued. "Deeply relaxed as you feel my hand pleasuring you. Everything is just fine. You want this. You need this. You need to surrender to me." The words faded again, replaced by the language of soft skin against hard flesh.

"Oh god," he groaned.

Katie's words came delicately. "Close your eyes."

Obediently, his eyelids descended shutting out the world in favour of Katie's manipulations. "You are so, so, relaxed," she said gently. "Everything is just right. Slowly, ever so slowly… " She breathed while her hand guided his arousal. "Turn around and face me, David. Your eyes are still closed. You feel so, utterly, utterly, beautifully relaxed."

"Yes," he replied. He turned to her, his eyes shut, a pleasant smile upon his round, handsome face. His stiff penis pressed against her stomach. Its heat and hardness felt good, and she took him in both hands, gently caressing him with splayed fingers; teasing, not stroking, pressing his foreskin downwards, exposing his tip, before releasing him.

Her hands danced upwards, over his stomach to his chest. She kissed him, pressing delicately against his lips. Then, in a light breath that floated like moonlight washing over him, she whispered, "David. Accept me."

"Yes," he whispered.

She kissed him again and he pushed against her, offering a litany of sweet kisses to Katie's full lips. Reluctantly, she forced herself away, trailing over new stubble and descending to his neck.

Her hands scribed swirling patterns over his strong thighs. They brushed inwards, teasing and tormenting his member, her sharp fingernails grating his foreskin, making him gasp from the unexpected pain.

"Relax," she breathed, as her long incisors grazed across his neck in search of the vein. When she found it, she snatched his cock firmly in her hand and stroked him, vigorously this time, as though she were determined to bring him to a swift and healthy ejaculation.

David offered a satisfying gasp and pushed against her, eagerly matching her movements with hip thrusts.

Katie's desire ruptured throughout her body. She was on him instantly, legs apart, his hard phallus pressed against her hot pussy, restrained only by the thin veil of her cotton briefs.

As her cunt ground against him, her teeth penetrated his body, rupturing the skin and slicing into the vein. Hot blood oozed as her tongue lapped hungrily at the invigorating heat that spurted from his neck.

David groaned, emitting a deep, almost orgasmic gasp. Katie's rhythm increased, her juices soaking through cotton and coating his cock as she rubbed herself against him. She felt him thrusting vigorously, desperate to break the artificial hymen that prevented him from sliding into her.

As she gulped his spectral energy, a rush of power swept through her. Her body tingled, invigorated by the purified waves of spiritual strength.

His eyes shot open, pupils wide like black pearls. An unasked question formed upon his lips as he tried to rise. Katie pressed her hands against his shoulders. "Relax," she soothed, his fresh blood coating her chin. It dripped onto his chest, trailing lines like tributaries from a river. "Relax, relax." She lifted herself up, pulled her underwear aside and slid onto him, planting him deep within her. His blood marred her smile, glossing her teeth and lips.

"Watch me," she said, sliding gently upwards until only his tip nudged against her wet opening. She hovered there, tempting and teasing as she pushed against him. Her words transformed into a hypnotic whisper. "Watch me."

Obediently, he stared up at her smooth face, flushed pink with his blood.

"Good boy." Katie slid down onto his rigid phallus, stretching every second into eternity as she filled herself with his length. He felt good, flooding her with a satisfying warmth. She climbed again, picking up speed until she was pistoning against him. Then she returned to his neck, gorging on his blood. Energy pulsed through her body, stimulating fibres and chemicals as her orgasm approached.

She moved faster against him, riding and draining as she pumped his energy from his groin and stole it through his neck. Her orgasm exploded, unleashing wave upon wave of pure and rejuvenating energy. She took one last taste of his hot, fresh blood, then, filled with his power, she lifted herself off his swollen member.

He groaned, his rigid cock trembling on the edge of orgasm as she left him, hard and unsatisfied.

She redressed quickly and stepped back into her heels, then kissed him and whispered into his ear. "Good boy. You're not allowed to cum. You save it for me."

"Who are you?" he asked.

"Your new mistress," she replied. "Remember my name: Katie." Then she disappeared from his room.

Chapter Seven

Kurt was finding things difficult. He'd only been serving for two days and already he wanted his clothes on and his cage off. There had been no indication of Tanya's presence and he was beginning to think that there was nothing to learn here. Tanya had simply arranged a party for these fetishists and then disappeared into the night to start a new life somewhere without him.

Lost in his self-reprimanding thoughts, he nearly dropped the cutlery he was setting out upon the oak table when Emma slipped into the dining room. "How was it?" the well-spoken woman asked, closing the door behind her.

The simple innocence of Emma's flirtatious enquiry ignited Kurt's frustrated arousal, placing it front and centre in conjunction with the blue cage that sat snuggly above his balls. Unseen, beneath the plastic sheath, his cock twitched into life. An erection stifled by the hard casing. He decided to keep his concentration focused on the places at the table.

"Are you flustered?" Emma enquired.

"Me? No." Still, he didn't look up.

Emma leant back, provocatively thrusting her breasts forward against the loose material of her grey T-shirt. "You're not the first boy we've had serving us naked, Kurt. Or locked in chastity."

His face turned red. His hand hovered over the table, uncertain where to place the next item.

"Am I putting you off?"

"No." *Yes*.

"So, how is it?"

"It's tight," he said, still avoiding her gaze. His reflection formed a vague shape on the polished cutlery. He placed the knife clumsily, almost dropping it. It pivoted, its tip coming to a stop in Emma's direction. He glanced briefly at the pretty woman and her eyes flashed with amusement. His dropped to the table and he repositioned the item carefully, setting it vertically beside the dinner knife.

Emma responded humorously. "Tight?"

Kurt nodded. *For God's sake, don't ask me. Can't you just leave? God, I want to fuck you. Let me out of this cage and you'll see how I really feel.* Mentally, he shook his head. *What the hell are they doing to me? Tanya, where are you? Look what I've done for you. I need to ask her about Tanya.*

He retreated to the other side of the table, away from the staring blonde. His lower half hidden behind the tall curved backs of the chairs.

Emma pushed off from the door. She stopped opposite him. "Kurt. You don't have to worry."

"I'm not worried," he lied.

"Why are you hiding then?"

"I'm laying the table."

"Do you want to leave?"

"Leave?"

"Return to your old, dull, lonely life," she pressed. "I could tell Katie that I don't think you'll work out."

The young man shook his downcast head. His fingers tightened on the cutlery. He released it, gently setting it in place, and clutched the back of the chair.

"I know you want this, Kurt," Emma said. "You'd have gone the second you read Katie's note. You'd have come out of that room. Your clothes still on. Soggy sock still squelching..." She smiled. "I'd have taken you back upstairs and you'd have left. Back to your empty house. To your broken dreams. To that despair that lives in you." She watched him closely. His strong jaw clenching and unclenching, pulsing like an anxious heart, in time with his fingers. "But you didn't. You stayed. You stripped. You went into that room and you met her. You met Katie. You met something, someone so different. Someone that touched you deeply. So deeply that you'd do anything to experience that again, wouldn't you? That's why you are here. Naked and locked in chastity. Ready and eager to serve us. To serve Katie, your mistress."

Kurt sighed. He looked up at her at last and shook his head. "I don't know what I'm doing."

"You need this. No matter how much that big male ego tries to tell you that you don't. The simple fact is, you do. You need this."

He shrugged. *I need this? No, Emma,* he thought, *I need to know what happened to my fiancée.* He visualised Katie's name scribbled in Tanya's handwriting on a scrap of paper that he'd found in Tanya's coat pocket after her disappearance. That, along with the information gleaned from the woman at the events agency that had hired Tanya to arrange the party, were the two leads that had brought him to this place.

He backed away from the table, far enough to expose his sheathed groin.

Emma stared at it. "I know you like it," she asserted. "It turns you on. Knowing we have the key. Knowing that we have that power over you."

Does it? he thought, despite the undeniable increase of heat down below.

She moved around the table, a solitary finger tracing over the curved backs of the chairs. "That very, sensual, sexual power over your dick. Now, tell me," she said as she stopped before him, "how was last night?" She folded her arms.

Kurt swallowed. "There's not much to say. I dropped her off and picked her up. That's about it. I sat in the car for the rest of it."

"She must have said something," Emma probed. "She always talks about them."

"Not to me." He returned to the cutlery, adjusted the angle of one of the ornate knives, then picked up the others and continued to lay the table. "She tells you what she does?"

"I'm her pet, she tells me lots of things," Emma confirmed.

"Her pet? What does that mean, exactly?" *Did that happen to Tanya? Taken as a pet then killed as Katie exhibited her true nature? Just ask her.*

Emma pressed her tongue between her teeth and top lip. "Exactly, it means I'm her girlfriend, her lover, and *your* boss."

"I don't see the point," Kurt said, moving to the next seat.

"What do you mean?"

"Not you," he clarified, opting to face his predicament head on. *Maybe I can argue my way out of this chastity thing.* "I mean, why I'm naked and in chastity."

"Katie feeds on blood, right," Emma said. "You got that?"

His eyes narrowed. "Does she?"

"She fed on you."

"Er, yeah, I couldn't really miss it." He touched the two marks on the side of his neck. "Tell me then..." He put the cutlery down in the centre of the placemat and looked at her again. "Are you her only pet, or does she have lots of women at her beck and call? You said that men and women come and go..."

"It's just me, at the moment," Emma replied.

"And in the past?"

Emma's lips were tight. Her eyes narrowed as she studied him as though searching for a deeper, unasked question. "There were others."

Kurt tried his best to maintain a casualness to the conversation as if he were barely interested. "Were?" His attention returned to the table, tilting his head as he eyed the alignment of cutlery.

Emma nodded.

"Did you meet them?" He adjusted a knife, stood up and studied its position before readjusting it once more.

"I've met some," Emma said. "I already told you, women come and go, just like servers."

"Go where?"

"Depends. Most go home. Sometimes they go to other sisters, sometimes they are turned, and sometimes they just...go."

"You mean..." He stared at her again, wondering how much she was withholding. "They're killed?"

"People die all the time," she replied.

"Did you ever meet a woman called Tanya?" he asked, elated that he had finally found the words to his thoughts.

The blonde's face was calmly placid. "Is that the name of your fiancée?"

Kurt stared at her in stunned silence.

"That was her name, wasn't it, Tanya?"

"Do you know where she is?"

"Hand on my heart," she said, making the gesture, "I don't. Tell me about her."

"No," he said, closing down at the thought of making small talk about Tanya for Emma's amusement.

"Fair enough." She shrugged. "You should concentrate on yourself, anyway."

"Why?" he snapped. "Did Katie kill Tanya?"

"Kurt, I honestly don't know anything about Tanya." Emma's tone was sincere. "You are here now. Focus on yourself. You are Katie's server. Lots of men will be so jealous of you."

"What, of me being her slave?"

"You're not a slave, you're a server; Katie's server."

"Is that it?"

"That's a better life than many men will ever get, especially with the benefits Katie brings."

"Benefits?" Kurt shook his head. "Being naked and in chastity doesn't feel like a benefit."

"Give it time."

"What about the male vampires?" he queried, watching her closely. "Do they have naked women serving them?"

"I've never met one."

"But they're around?"

Emma shrugged again. "I've never met one."

"Hmm," he murmured, frustrated by the blonde's inability to answer his questions. "And all of this?" His gaze dropped to his groin and he shook his head. "I mean...what the hell, look at me. This is ridiculous."

"This isn't a joke, Kurt. Katie needs blood to survive, but she can also live off energy. You know, like an energy vampire; psychic vampire. You boys waste a lot of energy," she made a wanker sign with her hand. "Especially young men like you." She grinned. "She's basically put a stop cock on your cock."

"A stop cock on my cock," Kurt repeated. He laughed at the strangeness of it all and picked up the cutlery again.

"It's stopped you, hasn't it?"

"It's too tight." He shook his head, as if denying what had happened to him. "Look, I don't want to talk about it." He concentrated on the placings then adjusted a knife and set down a spoon to form a horizontal line that contrasted with the verticals. "How many did you say there would be?" he asked, counting out the places.

"Four: Katie, Amy, Evie, and Aadhira."

Four, he thought. Their spoken names brought his worst fears to life. *I've not even adjusted to this new world and already there's going to be others.* His heart thumped angrily in his chest. A ball of anxiety screaming to be left alone.

"What about you?"

"Pets don't share tables with vampires when they have guests, unless we're told to."

"Where do you eat then?"

"In here, sometimes, or the kitchen, one of the other rooms, my bedroom. It depends."

"No one else tonight? Any pets?"

"Not here. The servers will help you. The pets, if there are any, won't need places. They'll eat elsewhere." She grinned and winked.

Kurt's heart sunk like a ship swallowed by a tidal wave. *What if Tanya turns up? Alive. Reborn in the image of Katie or another vampire.*

"Anyway," Emma continued, "I don't think Amy and Aadhira have pets any more, and, between you and me, Evie's probably scared hers off. She can be a bit intense."

"So, no pets?" he asked.

"I don't think so."

"And no men?"

"As I said, like you, the men will be serving the women." She grinned again. "Just as it should be. They'll be naked and in chastity as well, so you don't need to worry about being the odd one out."

"Right. Okay, thanks," Kurt said, feeling a little comfort from her words. He counted out the places and decided to move the position he'd laid out to the other side of the table.

"I'd really like to know about her," Emma said.

"About who?" he asked, cautiously.

Emma watched Kurt shift the placemat. "The woman you are desperate to find; your fiancée."

"My fiancée," he repeated, as he pulled the spare seat away from the table and placed it temporarily beside the wall.

"Yes."

"What was her name? Tanya?"

He stared at Emma, hoping to catch a reaction that might indicate a little more than mild curiosity. "Yes. Tanya."

"Tanya," Emma repeated, without any trace of emotion. She grabbed the spare chair and spun it around so its back was facing Kurt. "So, what happened?"

This is your chance, Kurt thought, as his lips tightened. He took a long, tiresome breath, inhaling the conditioned air. "I thought *you* might be able to tell me that."

Emma slipped down onto the seat, her legs parted, arms resting on its back. "Me?" She shook her head. "I don't know anything. So, what happened?"

"You don't know?" he countered.

Emma shook her head. "No."

"She organised a party for Katie."

"When?"

"About six months ago and then she left."

"What? That's it?"

"What do you mean?" he asked, watching her closely.

"She left," Emma noted, without any sign of subterfuge. *She looks curious.* "She did."

"And you think she's here?"

"You tell me," he challenged.

"I never met her," Emma said, "and if she walked out on you then you need to forget her."

"I can't. She's my fiancée."

"Who left you. Kurt, you need to move on. Katie doesn't like negativity to get in the way."

"In the way of what?"

"Her life. She's lasted this long, she doesn't need downers. She needs uppers."

"Are you an upper?" he asked.

She grinned, mischievously. "You have no idea how much of an upper I can be."

"I bet," he agreed, averting his gaze from the curly blonde. He scanned the table, trying to remain professional. "And her to you? I mean, if she really is a vampire...isn't she all take?"

"Everything has a price," Emma said, cryptically.

"What do you mean?"

"You'll find out. Anyway, you were telling me about your fiancée..."

"You just said I need to get over her," he shot back, feeling all the more certain that Emma knew nothing of any use.

"Talking helps. There's obviously more to it," she advised. "It's obvious there's more, so tell me what really happened. It'll help."

Kurt swallowed and shook his head tiredly, nevertheless, he answered, "She disappeared one night. We went to bed together and when I woke up she was gone. The front door was wide open, all her belongings were still in the house, but no Tanya."

"And you think Katie had something to do with it?"

Kurt sighed. He set down the final spoon and stared at her. "I found a slip of paper in Tanya's pocket with Katie's name on it. According to one of the women at the events agency she was Tanya's client."

"Katie doesn't tell me everything," Emma confessed.

Kurt studied her, wondering if she was just a great actress who was deliberately playing dumb or really knew nothing about his missing fiancée. "I thought you said she did."

With a twinkle in her eye, Emma whispered, "I exaggerated." When he said nothing, she added, "And you never heard from her again?"

He sighed. "I'm not doing this." He returned to the trolley, selected two cut crystal glasses and placed them on the right of the nearest two settings.

"You need to," Emma said.

"Don't play me, Emma," Kurt snapped. "She was involved with Katie. She organised a party for her, for Christ's sake. You must know something. You live with her!"

"A party?"

"For someone called Amy."

Emma's face remained dispassionate, her words calm and soothing. "And you think Katie...what, killed her?"

"Yes." Kurt paused then shook his head. "No. I don't know...maybe. She was involved with her and then she disappeared, in the middle of the night. Without a trace."

"I've never heard of her. The pet before me was called Jana."

"Is Emma your real name?"

"Yes. Katie's not interested in play names. Some of the other sisters might be, but I've never asked, not really thought about it, either."

"How long have you been her pet?"

"Two years."

"Two years." Kurt stared into empty space and frowned. "And you never met Tanya?"

Emma shook her head. "I had to go away for a few months due to a family illness, it's possible the party happened around then."

"Hmm. What about Katie's server who was here before me?"

"His name was Brook. He was a handsome man, tall – taller than you – and a bit bigger, too."

Kurt didn't ask whether she meant body or penis size. "Where is he?"

There was a finality to Emma's response when she shook her head. Her curls bounced from left to right.

"He's dead?"

"I didn't say that. You were going to get married, then?" she asked. "Did you have a date set? Arrangements made? Church or some special place? Or were you going to go abroad? I love a good wedding. So romantic and then you get to practice making babies..."

"Stop," he snapped. "I don't want to talk about it." He went to grab another glass, stopped himself and grasped the edge of the trolley instead. His fingers tightened until they turned white.

"Was she pregnant?" Emma soothed.

Kurt shook his head.

"Do you have a child?"

Kurt fell still.

"Kurt, you need to talk about it," Emma soothed. "It will help."

"No. I don't." He shoved the trolley away. It rolled towards the wall nearest to Emma. She stopped it before it impacted. "You'll feel better if you get it off your chest. Like when you emptied yourself in front of her."

"I said, don't."

"Maybe you just need to let it go. Whatever happened is done. Besides, you have a new life now."

"Stop it, Emma."

"No. You need to hear this. If she loved you, she'd have stayed. She left you, remember?"

"I said stop!" Kurt stormed out of the room, leaving the door half open.

She hurried after him, watching him disappear into the lift. It descended to his quarters and she waited for it to return then followed. She reached his door and knocked. "Kurt." He didn't answer. "Kurt. I'm sorry. Talk to me."

"Leave me alone," he called out. "I told you, I don't want to talk about it."

"That's fine, you don't have to. I'm sorry if I made you feel bad. Come on, let's go outside. Get some fresh air."

He offered a mock laugh. "It's freezing."

"You can wear some clothes, silly. Katie won't mind. Come on. Come and get some fresh air with me."

He didn't answer immediately, and Emma considered leaving when the door opened. His eyes looked red. "Come on," she said, sympathetically. "Fresh air will help."

Chapter Eight

It was a cold afternoon. Forced by gusting winds, sporadic rain fell in heavy waves. "It's chilly," Emma said, sliding her arm through Kurt's.

"Yeah," he agreed, glad to be wearing clothes once more. It highlighted the strange and unexpected shift between his usual, fashionable yet practical attire, and Katie's expectation that he remained nude from now on. He couldn't deny that Emma was right; there *was* an exhibitionist pleasure to being naked for them, though despite Tanya's humorous proposition one drunken night early on in their relationship (which he had strenuously dismissed before taking her to the bedroom and giving her the pounding she needed), he'd never done anything like it before. He didn't want to admit his arousal at being naked to the attractive blonde. The chastity cage, however, quashed the enjoyment dramatically. "Where are we going?"

"For a walk," she replied, leading him away from the bungalow.

"I thought you said it's not safe?"

"Safe?"

"When I first came here, you told me there were problems..."

"Oh, yeah, well..." Emma scanned the long, grassy grounds. "I think we'll be okay. Maybe just don't tell Katie."

"Hold on." He pointed his body away from her, dropped his hand between his legs, and adjusted his chastity device.

"You alright?" she asked, grinning.

"Sometimes it catches the skin, if I'm not careful."

"Ouch."

"Yes, ouch," he agreed. The wind gusted as they set off once again, now, thankfully, minus the rain. He ruffled his collar and tightened it around his neck. "Thanks for the clothes."

"The jeans look good on you," Emma said.

"The shoes are expensive," he noted.

"Katie wants us all to look classy."

"I didn't think Katie wanted me to wear anything."

"That's for indoors. That's the general rule, but this is England. We've got to be pragmatic," Emma said. "It must be weird for you, not wearing clothes."

"It is."

"Yet you took the job."

"Did I?"

"Didn't you?" she asked, as they stepped onto the road.

"Left or right?" he asked.

She checked both directions. "Left. There's a big old tree at Gibbets Cross where they used to hang criminals."

"I didn't take you for the macabre type."

"I live with a vampire, how macabre do you want?" Emma countered.

He shook his head.

"What?"

"What you just said."

"What?" Her smile warmed her face. Her soft cheeks were rosy.

"That I live with a vampire?"

"I still don't know if I believe it isn't some kind of elaborate performance art or fetishistic roleplay."

"You were there. She drank your blood, didn't she? Anyway, I want you to know that I am here to help. I may be your keyholder, but you can confide in me and if I can, I'll do my best to help you get some closure."

He stared at her long and hard. Her pretty face looked pleasant and sincere. "Thanks."

"Do you really think that Tanya was here?" Emma asked.

Kurt shrugged. "Maybe, maybe not, but she *was* hired by Katie."

"And you just happened to find her address on the internet and turn up for an interview?"

"Like I said, Tanya had been hired by an events agency to arrange a party for high-end clientele," Kurt explained. "I was really happy, because after it happened—"

"It happened?"

Kurt nodded.

"What happened?" Emma asked.

Kurt sighed. He stared up as the rain began to tumble down again.. He swallowed and took a deep breath of cold air. "Tanya lost...we lost our baby girl, Lotte. Respiratory distress syndrome – RDS, they call it – pneumonia. After we lost Lotte, I lost Tanya." He glanced at Emma, his face a graveyard of memories. "Emotionally, I mean. She closed down; fell into a deep depression. I lost her and couldn't..." His words choked up in his throat. "Bollocks," he hissed and shook his head violently. "Sorry. Give me a minute."

"Take your time," Emma soothed.

"No," he asserted. "I'm alright. I couldn't pull her out of it. I didn't know what to do. I avoided it. I avoided her. When she was hired to plan the party, I thought that Chavvi, her friend at the events agency, had broken through to her. She was suddenly motivated again. It was a complete turn around. I hadn't seen her like that in such a long time.

"Anyway, the party happened, somewhere, I don't know where; Tanya never said, and she returned home on such a high. I thought she was through it. I mean, she *was* through it, I think. She was just so elated. She told me how magical it all was. How utterly different from anything she'd ever experienced before. She didn't mention vampires or naked servers or pets or any of it. She was practically floating with joy. I was stunned I guess, because, as I said, I'd not seen her so happy since before we lost Lotte. We even made love, something we'd not done in, well, months."

He gritted his teeth as he reflected on the pain of their final moments. "After Lotte had died Tanya would wake up in the middle of the night and go downstairs. I'd find her there, rocking back and forth, a cushion in her arms. I'd ask her to come back to bed but she'd just ignore me. It made me frustrated but I never got cross with her, never raised my voice or anything. I just... I didn't know what to do. I just wanted her to snap out of it, to come back to me so that we could start again. But she was lost. I didn't know what to do." He wiped his eyes, less any tears break through his thick exterior.

Kurt took a long, deep breath. "The following night she disappeared. When I awoke I thought she was downstairs in her armchair again. I expected to see her, rocking back and forth, the cushion squeezed tightly in her arms. Instead, her chair was empty, the cushion was on the floor, the front door was open, and she was gone. I've not seen or heard from her since. Something happened at that party. Something that affected her. It brought her out of herself, long enough for us to be normal again, but then...then she was gone. Someone knows what happened. I'm sure of it."

He fell silent, embracing the gusting wind that directed branches like an erratic composer conducting an orchestra. The rain scored his face but failed to extricate him of painful memory. Droplets merged to stream down his stubbled face. "Chavvi, the woman at the events agency, told me about Katie's advert for a server. She knew I was desperate for an answer and wanted to help me get closure." He shook his head again. "I'm sorry."

"Don't apologise," Emma said. "That sounds horrid for both of you and she sounds as though she needed some expert help."

"I know, but she refused to see a doctor or therapist or anyone. She blamed them, I did too, but now, looking back, I don't think it was anyone's fault."

"So, you think Katie knows where she is?" Emma asked.

"I don't know. Maybe. I don't know what to say to her. I was going to ask her last night but..." He paused. "Katie's something else, I lost my nerve."

"She is something else." Emma nodded in agreement.

"Can we change the subject. It's a bit heavy talking about this."

"Of course."

"Thanks. Were there many others that went for the job?"

"You were the first," Emma said. "She chose you."

"No one else applied?"

"They did, but she wanted you."

"Why?"

"Does it matter? It's obvious you're an exhibitionist."

"An exhibi..." Kurt laughed the comment off.

"Aren't you?"

"There's something intense about it, for sure. Especially when I'm in the presence of a pretty woman," he confessed.

"I'm Katie's, not yours. Besides, your dick's safely locked away."

"Yeah, not much fun in that. I'm sorry."

"Why be sorry?"

"Tanya."

"She left you. Remember that, Kurt. She left *you*. You were there, even if you didn't know what to do, but she was the one that left you. No notes or anything, right?"

Kurt shook his head.

"Well, now you're here. This is your life. You do realise that you may be better off not knowing what happened to her?"

"What do you mean?"

"Nothing sinister," Emma affirmed. "She may have just started again. Somewhere else, and besides, you need to remember that you are Katie's server now."

"I guess," he said, feeling as though he had one foot in both worlds. "But it's not going to be much fun if I'm forced to be in chastity."

"I already told you, silly, it's not forever. There's lots of fun when she lets you out – *if* she lets you out," Emma replied. "Lot's of fun; for us, anyway." She pulled away from him and shook her head. Droplets of water sprinkled the air from the trees above, a few catching Kurt.

"When will she?" he asked.

Emma grinned. "What? Let you out?"

He grunted a confirmation.

"Depends if you're a good boy." Her hand reached to her chest, dipped below her jacket, and pulled out a key.

"You have my key?"

"One of them." She looked proud and held it tantalisingly before him for a moment, then popped it back beneath her clothes.

Kurt hesitated, then asked, "Can I have it?"

She frowned, incredulous at his naively hopeful question. "No."

"What if I need to..."

"Need to?"

"You know...get out."

Emma stared straight ahead, a triumphant grin upon her face. "You'll have to ask Katie."

"Why've you got it then?"

"Katie isn't always around." Her grin widened. "Are you feeling nervous?"

"I don't know..." he mused.

"You must have some idea?"

"The cage is tight. It's uncomfortable when I sleep."

"Yet you chose to accept it."

"I did," he admitted. "If it means I'll find out what happened to Tanya."

"Katie's unlike any woman you've ever known," Emma said, avoiding a stream of water that coursed across the centre of the road.

"Yeah, she's something else. I don't know what I'd have done if she'd decided to send me away."

"You didn't go to the police?"

"Police?"

"About Tanya?" Emma replied.

"They logged Tanya as a missing person. Otherwise, apart from the note, the agency and the party, there were no leads. Someone, somewhere, must know something. Sometimes I think there's been a cover up – powerful people in powerful places because the police should have come here and asked questions. Unless," he stared at her, "did they?"

"No, no police. Did you tell them about us?"

"Yes, of course. They said they'd already spoken to everyone of interest and had reached a dead end." He chuckled sourly.

"What's funny?" Emma said.

"Dead end; apt for a vampire, I guess."

"Yes," Emma agreed, and smiled.

They walked on in silence. Scaring away the few birds that rested among the gnarled branches of barren trees.

"This is it," Emma said as they came to an isolated crossroads. An old oak, thick with rough bark and heavy branches, stood on one corner. Its aged arms stuck out like a disfigured cross pending a crucifixion. "Gibbets Cross." High hedges, weathered and balding, lined the sides of the old country road that dissected their route. A plateau of twigs and mud coated its centre; evidence of their distance from busier thoroughfares.

"How times change," Kurt said, as they slipped around the corner to avoid the gusting wind.

"For us," Emma agreed.

"Do you think she turned Tanya?"

"No. Katie wouldn't turn someone she hired to plan a party. I know her well enough to know she wouldn't do that."

"Then, what the hell happened?" he asked.

"I don't know, Kurt. I really don't know. Like I say, I was away for a few months, it was probably around the time of the party."

"She never mentioned a party to you?"

Emma shook her head.

"Is she going to turn you? Does she turn pets?"

Emma shrugged. "Come on, let's get back before we get too wet. Hot showers all round."

"When are the guests arriving?" he asked, rapidly changing the subject so that he didn't have to think of Emma in a shower.

"Not until late. Probably nine or ten. Margarita's coming around six."

"Margarita?"

"She's the cook and she doesn't take any shit. So be prepared."

"I thought you might be cooking."

"Don't be silly. You'll like Margarita. She's Bulgarian. Her food is delicious. Three Michelin stars delicious."

"Ah, okay," Kurt said, feeling nervous at the addition of another lady into the mix. "How long has she worked for Katie?"

"Fifteen years or more. Katie poached her from a top restaurant in London. I'm not sure which one."

"So, she's seen a lot of people come and go?"

"She's used to naked servers, if that's what you mean, so don't worry. She's seen it all and much, much more."

"And pets?"

"She doesn't like us," Emma said. "She thinks we're hangers on. Wannabes that Katie should get rid of."

Kurt's interest raised along with his eyebrows.

"She won't know anything about Tanya, if that's what you're thinking. She just... thinks we're in the way. She's probably jealous. You know how some women can be."

Their journey home was quiet, narrated only by the meditative patter of rain. Kurt's mind flitted from thoughts of Emma in the shower, alone or with the addition of Katie and then himself, to an all-consuming hunger for Tanya's return. It buried any desire for the pretty blonde, smothering the potency of hot fantasies by replacing them with memories of romance and intimacy with his fiancée. He pictured Tanya, lazing on the sofa as she waited for his return from his interview with Katie. He'd kick off his shoes, dump his keys on the side and coat on the hook, and kiss her. Kiss her as if the love of every man and every woman that had ever lived had merged into their embrace. He'd tell her about the strangest interview of his life. Watch her laugh as he told her what was expected of him.

"You didn't become her naked butler?" she'd ask.

His response would be incredulous. A denial that covered a tiny deceit. Part of him had wanted to. "No way."

"You can strip for me," she'd challenge. "The house needs hoovering."

He'd laugh. Kiss her again. Hold her tight. Feel her curves against him. Press his manhood against her. Feel it swell as their lips touched.

The frustrating effects of his cage unwound the imagined scenario as they entered the grounds.

"Make sure you're ready to answer the door for Margarita," Emma advised. "She doesn't like to be kept waiting."

"What time are you—"

"I'll be around later," she replied, entering the security pin. "A bit before Katie. Before our guests."

"Okay."

"Clothes off as soon as we're inside," she instructed. "Katie's boots will need cleaning. She'll want a pair for later, so clean them all while you're waiting for Margarita."

"This feels very strange," Kurt confessed.

"Don't lie," Emma replied. "I know you're enjoying it. Katie wouldn't have chosen you otherwise." The door opened. Emma crossed the threshold first followed by Kurt, who wondered what the evening was going to be like and hoping that he'd glean some information about Tanya's disappearance.

Chapter Nine

Margarita was a round lady in her later years. A little over 5-foot, she arrived with a bag over one shoulder and a chip on the other. Kurt wasn't sure about her, but he reckoned she'd started as she meant to go on, shoving her bag into his arms and barraging him with orders, then telling him to hurry up when he wasn't fast enough. He closed the door behind her, severing the snap of cold that followed her into the bungalow.

"Come," she said, already halfway down the corridor. "Hurry up." She stopped at the lift, turned around and watched him as he finalised the locking procedure. There was no attempt to avert her gaze as he approached. Her smile was garnished with sadistic delight. "What is your name?"

"Kurt, Miss Dachkov," he said, feeling particularly self-conscious as he pressed the lift call.

"Hmm," she murmured, studying him like an agent of the Bulgarian Intelligence Service.

"I'm the new butler."

"Server," she corrected.

"Miss Katie told me to assist you tonight."

"You better not be as lazy as Edward." The lift pinged. Behind her the door parted. Anticipating her movement, Kurt stalled, falling onto his tiptoes when she remained still. His naked form towered over her. Margarita's hand snapped like a viper. Her meaty fingers locked around his balls. He fell back onto his heels, leaning into her as the cook's fleshy fingers tightened. "Do not get in my way," she warned, staring up at him. "Do not make me tell you things two times. Do what I tell you, when I tell you. And do not get this..." she squeezed harder, "near my food. You wear an apron in my kitchen. I do not need to see this or – cage or not – I will mistake it for tiny sausage, chop it up and add to food."

"I'll do my best, Miss Dachkov," he replied through gritted teeth.

"You do better than your best." Her fingers tightened.

Kurt yelped. His shoulders hunched, bringing his face intimately close to hers. "Yes, Miss," he murmured. His stomach muscles constricted like levers activated by the pressure on his testicles. "I will. I will."

She held him for a few moments longer.

"Please," he groaned.

Her grip slackened, fleshy forefinger and thumb switched to ring his ball sack. "You call me cook. I'm not a chef, not any more. Now I am the cook. You call me cook; Cook Margarita. You understand?"

"Yes, Cook Margarita."

She released him with a jolt and wiped her hands on the sides of her long skirt.

Kurt thought the lift dropped a little as she stepped in. He followed her and pressed the button to the floor below.

Cook Margarita was a whirlwind in the kitchen, moving with the unexpected precision of a gymnast. She shooed Kurt from her patch, ordering him to find an apron so she didn't get distracted by his sheathed penis. He hurried off, glad to be away from the Bulgarian behemoth, in search of the required garment.

By the time the guests arrived, some time after ten, Cook Margarita had created a banquet of food. Emma popped in briefly to see how things were going, taking a moment to admire Kurt's tight, black and white check apron and forcing him to do a twirl so she could enjoy the sight of his pert backside. Katie remained absent.

The first two guests arrived simultaneously. Miss Evie and Miss Aadhira were announced by Evie's server, Edward, who stepped aside to enable the two vampires to enter. Kurt eyed them both with interest, wondering if they'd had anything to do with Tanya's disappearance. He was quickly lost in the drama of their arrival, which forced a stop to any investigative enquiry.

Evie was the louder of the two, with a broad frame and an unabashed personality. She took her time to inspect Katie's new server, instructing him to remove his apron and turn around.

"Cook Margarita told me to wear the apron for the evening," Kurt replied, unsure which of the two feelings – humiliated or flattered – was more dominant. He opted to focus on flattery. "I feel obliged to do as she requested."

"You feel obliged to do as she requested?" Evie repeated, pushing Kurt's shoulder and forcing him into a 180. "What do you think, Addy? Good arse? Or is he just another ass?" She laughed and gave Kurt a sharp slap on the backside that made him jump.

Aadhira rolled her brown eyes. "Don't worry about her," she advised. "She always has to touch."

"And you don't?" Evie challenged.

Kurt stared at the fangs exposed by Aadhira's grin, trying to decipher false teeth from the real thing. As far as he could tell, if they were not the real deal they were perfectly crafted additions.

"Oh my god," Aadhira said. Her eyes narrowed as she studied Kurt, her face becoming visibly nauseated. She glanced at her companion. "She's done it again. His energy centres are off. He's like dirty washing-up water."

"Always taking the charity cases," Evie noted, staring down her nose at Kurt. "She fed, too. He's got bite marks. At least he's fit."

"Urgh," Aadhira groaned. "Come on." She led the other vampire to the lift, leaving Kurt to wait for Evie's server who'd slipped into the washroom to change.

When Edward reappeared, he was naked and cock locked.

"You too," Kurt said.

"What?" Edward asked, rather gruffly.

"They put you in chastity."

"Oh, yeah. It's alright. I get let out a lot." He grinned and winked. "Miss Evie likes to play."

"I don't get it," Kurt said. "I mean, what's the point?"

"The point?" Edward asked, strolling down the hallway as if he owned the place.

"Of making us do this?" Kurt hurried along, trying to match Edward's pace.

"You'll have to ask Miss Katie." Edward shrugged, waiting for the lift to return.

"How long have you..." The front door bell rang again and Kurt made his way back, leaving a disinterested Edward to make his own way down.

Of the three vampires that attended, Amy had the greatest presence and was of the greatest interest to Kurt. Her height matched Cook Margarita's one and a half metres. Her frame was slender like Aadhira's, with more pronounced curves that were partially obscured by a pinstriped trouser suit. In place of a collar and tie she wore a low cut white T-shirt with a visible key hanging from a gold necklace.

Beyond an outfit that conveyed a smart and confident businesswoman, there was a depth to her unlike anything Kurt had ever experienced. He tried to comprehend what made her so different; the intense gaze that pressed intrusively into him or the weighted inertia that seeped from her presence and left him feeling that a megaton bomb might explode at any moment. Either way, Kurt found Amy to be uniquely intriguing. He wondered if this woman had played a significant part in Tanya's disappearance.

"Good evening, Miss Amy," he said.

Her gaze was a cold wind blowing across an arctic steppe. Kurt shivered. *So this is what a gazelle feels like before a lioness is about to eat it,* he mused.

"Take my coat," she said, removing the long, black garment that was draped over her shoulders.

"Of course, Miss," Kurt replied, folding it over his arm. "Miss Katie is waiting downstairs."

"Miss Amy will make her own way down." It was Amy's handsome blonde server named Stefan who spoke, as he took Amy's coat from Kurt. He was dressed smartly in a tailor-made, blue suit.

"Very well," Kurt acknowledged, as the vampire proceeded along the well-trodden route. "Miss Evie and Miss Aadhira are already here."

Kurt watched Amy slip gracefully away, sensing that the answer he was seeking lay with the otherworldy creature that appeared as a beautiful woman. He wanted to shout after her: *What did you do? What happened? Where's Tanya? What have you done with her?*

Amy stepped into the lift and spun slowly around until she was facing him. Her mesmerising blue eyes waned as though dusk had fallen. They drew Kurt towards her, enticing him to dive deep into their cold, nocturnal depths.

She knows, he realised. *She knows what happened. Where is she? Where's Tanya?* He took a preparatory breath, his question about to be verbalised. The lift doors closed like a guillotine on his inquiry, and the lift descended.

"We saw Miss Evie's car," Stefan said. "Did she come with Miss Aadhira?"

"She knows," Kurt said, ignoring the question.

"Knows?" Stefan queried.

Kurt stared at the lift doors. "Amy – Miss Amy – knows what happened...to Tanya."

Stefan shook his head. "Tanya?"

"You've got to help me," Kurt said, suddenly facing Stefan. "Please. My fiancée's missing. Katie hired her to arrange a party for Amy."

Stefan frowned. "A party?"

"About six months ago. You must know something. You are her server, aren't you?"

"Yes, yes I am and there was a party, a private party, but I do not recall anyone called Tanya being there," Stefan said. "And you need to be careful throwing accusations around here."

"Is that a threat?"

"It's a friendly warning." Stefan sounded sincere. His young face serious but not threatening.

"Shit," Kurt said finally. "How the hell do I find out?"

"Whatever you do," Stefan said, "take some more friendly advice: be careful who you start accusing."

"What's tonight all about?" Kurt asked. "Katie's not told me anything."

"Just a get together. The sisters have them now and then, not often. How long have Miss Evie and Miss Aadhira been here?"

"Not very," Kurt said, trying to shelve his pressing desire to challenge Amy. "They arrived with a server called Edward."

"Okay. Wait for me, will you? I'll just get changed, then we can head down."

"You're serving as well?" Kurt checked as he commenced the lock up process once again. "Emma – Katie's pet – said there would be other servers, but Cook Margarita was a bit vague. I thought there might be pets, too."

"Pets? No, not tonight," Stefan answered. "Only Emma as far as I know. As for servers: We may just wait until Cook Margarita calls us. Sometimes, we're needed to do other things."

"Other things?" Kurt sealed the house once more.

Stefan shook his head as if the question were too vast to be answered. "It could be anything. Anything at all. I'll just be a moment."

He was. He popped in and out, stark naked, within a minute. His hairless body an illusion created by fine, blond hairs. "You're new, then," Stefan said, as they proceeded to the floor below.

"Very. My first service," Kurt said.

"You must have something Katie wants."

"What?"

"Katie usually wants something from her boys beyond mere service. Do you meditate?"

"Meditate? No."

"Are you celibate?"

"Er, no."

"Have you ever encountered a sister before?" Stefan enquired.

"I don't think so," Kurt replied. "Until a few days ago, I didn't even know they existed. I'm still not sure they do." His voice dropped to a whisper. "Is this real? I mean, like, real vampires?"

"You don't believe and you're Katie's server?"

"I don't know what to think."

"Well, she wants you for something. Maybe it's just because she thinks you're cute," Stefan suggested.

"I don't know." He contemplated telling Stefan more but decided to take the blond server's advice and be cautious.

They split up on the floor below. Stefan headed off in search of the sisters, while Kurt returned to the kitchen to see how Cook Margarita was doing. She remained busy and wanted none of his interference, forcing him out of the kitchen with a couple of accurate slaps on the backside from a well-aimed tea towel.

Kurt opted to bite the bullet and check in on Katie and her guests in the lounge. He knocked a couple of times, waited, and was about to enter when the door opened and Edward appeared. The aloof server immediately retreated to stand behind the sofa where Evie was playing a game on her phone and Aadhira was resting with her feet on her sister's lap.

Stefan was kneeling in front of Amy, who was seated on one of the two armchairs. Her left foot was stuck out in front of her, being expertly massaged by the naked blond. Her shoes were set neatly on the floor beside him.

The only other person present was Emma, who was standing behind Katie. She was dressed in a short, tight outfit that unveiled a sensual figure, making his pulse race. He forced himself to ignore her and focus on providing a professional, albeit unadorned, service to their guests.

"Is dinner ready?" Katie asked.

"It will not be too long, Miss," Kurt said, subtly studying Amy who returned the inspection with a penetrating gaze that bore through to the core of his pain. *Where is she?*

Amy remained frustratingly silent.

"Come back when it is ready." Katie dismissed him with a wave of her hand. "Emma, you can go too. I will call you later."

Emma nodded and quietly disappeared out of a side door.

"Hold on, Katie," Amy said. "I want to ask him some questions." Stefan's thumbs worked in unison over the ball of her foot, pressing firmly but gently over the flesh.

"Stay then," Katie said.

Kurt hesitated. *Questions,* he thought. *Yes, fine, only I've got some questions, too.*

"Come in," Katie said, beckoning with her arm.

He did as instructed and closed the door behind him.

"More," Katie said when Kurt lingered on the edge of the room. He took a few more steps, aware that all eyes, except Stefan's and Evie's, were on him.

"You are single, Kurt?" Amy asked.

Kurt swallowed. "I am, Miss."

"What is your sexual preference?"

"I am heterosexual. I like women," he answered.

"I understand something happened to your fiancée?" Amy continued.

Kurt glared at the back of Stefan's head. The server's attention remained seemingly oblivious on Amy's foot. "She disappeared, Miss," Kurt said, eyeing the sisters like a detective searching for the guilty party. Evie had yet to look up from her game. Aadhira stared at him through tight and inquisitive eyes. Edward did his best to not look bored while Katie adjusted her chair to study her server.

"Disappeared?" Amy enquired.

Kurt moistened his lips. "I was hoping one of you could answer that question, Miss."

"From the looks of your energy I thought she was dead," Aadhira declared.

Kurt glared at her. "Is she?"

There was a joyful malevolence to Evie's smile when she glanced up from her game, as though, already knowing the answer, she was keen to watch Kurt's reaction. "He's not happy."

"So what? He's a server, who cares how he feels," Katie said.

"*Was* she killed?" Amy asked, her gaze penetrating him to the core once again.

Kurt swallowed. "I... I don't know. She's missing. You might know her: Tanya Collins?"

"You came here with your accusations yet you do not really know what happened to her?" Amy stated. Stefan's attention moved to the centre of her sole, pressing inwards with his thumb.

"She was hired to arrange a party for you, Miss Amy, by Miss Katie. She returned home to me and then disappeared the following night. She took nothing with her and I've not seen or heard from her since. I was hoping that you – " he looked around the group, "one of you – might be able to tell me more."

"More?" Katie asked. "Like what?"

"Like who she might have befriended," Kurt said.

"Was she a pet?" Evie asked. Her fingers and thumbs tapped rapidly over the screen of her phone.

"She was a party planner," Kurt said.

"Miss," Katie sharply corrected.

"Miss," Kurt said.

"Did you drink from him?" Amy asked Katie.

"I did."

"Urgh," Aadhira groaned. "Dirty. His aura needs cleaning."

"Shut up, bitch," Katie snapped.

"Did you see anything?" Amy asked.

"Enough," Katie said. "He's not a natural server, but that was why I chose him. He'll be more fun than those boring slaves."

"And his fiancée?" Amy asked.

"He doesn't know," Katie said.

"What do you mean?" Kurt snapped.

The sisters fell silent and stared at Katie's server.

Katie screamed and shot from her chair. "How dare you speak to me like that!" She grabbed Kurt by the throat. He gasped as she slammed him against the door. Her knee shoved into his privates. His sheathed cock stabbed backwards into his balls.

Kurt clutched Katie's wrists and attempted to prise himself free. Her grip tightened.

"Kurt," Amy said calmly, "is another victim of that demon called love."

"Useless," Katie hissed. Her mouth parted in preparation for the bite. Her ivory-coloured incisors hung like frozen tears.

"Katie, wait," Amy said. "Help me understand, Kurt; you believe that your fiancée planned a party for me only to disappear shortly afterwards?"

Kurt nodded. "Please." Breathless, he tried to prise Katie's hands from his neck.

"Katie, let him speak," Amy instructed tiredly.

Katie's mouth snapped shut. She released his throat. Her knee still pressed against his groin, holding him in place. "Speak," she hissed.

"My fiancée, Tanya, was commissioned to arrange a party for Miss Amy," Kurt said, staring at Katie whose face remained intimately close. "She came home after the party but disappeared the following night. You are the best lead I have. The police got nowhere."

"I should punish you for this disrespect," the Russian vampire cautioned. "You are my server now. Your old life is dead."

"I'm just trying to find out what happened to her," Kurt protested.

"And you thought the best way to do that was to become Katie's server?" Amy asked.

"The lady at the agency suggested I go for a job interview. She said that because of the high-level of secrecy knocking on the door to your home and asking questions would get me nowhere."

"She did a good job," Evie said, "because now you're naked and vulnerable. We can do whatever we want to you."

"Yes, I know, Miss," he concurred. "I'm not here to cause you any problems. I'm just looking for—"

"No!" Katie snapped again. "You are my server!" She flipped him around. Hand on his wrist, pulling him from the door until she was behind him. Her arm wrapped across his throat, her fangs teasing his neck.

"Katie," Amy soothed. "Sit down."

"I can't believe you fed on him," Aadhira said, clearly unfazed by Katie's eruption.

Katie's grip remained tight until she groaned and released him, slapping his apron-covered cock cage as she returned to her seat. "Idiot."

Stefan moved on to Amy's heel.

"Tell him," Amy said as Katie sat down.

"Tell me?" Kurt asked, rubbing his neck. "Tell me what, Miss?"

"Later," Katie dismissed. "I'm hungry."

Despite the closed door, Margarita's voice bellowed along the hallway and into the room. "Boy! Boy! Boy!"

Evie looked up at him. "You're being called."

"Please, I need to know," Kurt said.

Katie's eye's deepened in her sockets. Her face fell into shadow. "You will do as you're told," she warned.

"Please, Miss," Kurt urged. "I need to know what happened to her."

"You need to serve your mistress," Amy advised.

"Boy! Boy! Boy!" came Margarita's echoing call again.

"I'll go," Edward said, and made to the door.

"No, Edward, Kurt will go," Evie ordered. "He can manage."

"Yes, Miss," Evie's server replied, barely able to conceal the irritation in his voice.

Kurt stared at the seated vampires, switching between Amy and Katie, hoping one of them would answer his question.

"Margarita is waiting," Katie said, her teeth grinding beneath a clenched jaw.

"Kurt, we will tell you what we know," Amy soothed. "But it is not wise to disobey your mistress."

He held his ground for another moment, ignoring their glares until finally, his chest rising and falling as he tried to calm his breathing, he reluctantly said, "Yes, Miss." He then spun around and walked briskly out of the room, closing the door behind him as another summons was shouted from the kitchen. "Boy!"

Kurt had just rounded the corner before Cook Margarita appeared in the doorway. "Come on," she said, backing away into the kitchen. "I have been calling you. Are you deaf as well as dumb?"

"Sorry, Cook Margarita," he replied, doing his best to refocus on the task in hand. Four starters were set out like fine art, their vibrant colours popping off the stoneware plates.

"Where are the other servers?"

"They have been told to wait, Cook Margarita," Kurt replied.

"Then you will serve them all," she said. "Do not drop them, or you will be licking the contents off the floor."

"I won't, Cook Margarita." Kurt scooped up the first two plates, then hurried back to the dining room where Stefan and Edward were helping the fours sisters into their seats.

"He'll be wondering through all of dinner service," Evie said. "Whatever happened to his fiancée. Hmm, I wonder..." She giggled, mischievously.

Kurt considered throwing the food in her face as he set the plate down in front of her.

"Evie, don't," Aadhira pleaded.

"He needs to ask Meghan," Evie said, between hungry mouthfuls. "That bitch knows."

Meghan, Kurt thought. *Who the hell is she?*

Chapter Ten

Kurt was quietly fuming through dinner service. Every now and then he caught Amy's eye, though the latter appeared not to notice. Beyond Evie's suggestion that he speak to Meghan – whoever the hell she was – the other vampires, including Katie, paid him no attention at all. It left him with time to ponder Katie and Amy's part in Tanya's disappearance and the identity of Meghan. From the way Evie spoke, he guessed she was a vampire, but until they said anything else, he could only surmise.

"We have nothing if we do not have their energy," Amy said from her seat at the head of the dining table. "I've told you that before, Aadhira."

"It feels cruel," Aadhira replied.

"There's nothing cruel about feeding," Evie said.

"That's not what I mean. I don't like to keep them locked up all the time."

"If you let him out, he'll show you no respect," Amy advised.

"I know that, I just mean—"

"Katie's didn't show any respect earlier," Evie noted.

"He's new, Evie," Katie hissed. "He'll learn."

"Like your last one?" Evie countered.

"Balance is important," Amy advised.

"I like them locked," Katie stated. "If I need to feed, I get a surge of power. A dam that is so full, almost to breaking point and..." She licked her lips, deliberately looking at the three servers. "I can feel how much they're about to pop. Break those fucking cock cages and show me how hard those dicks are for me."

"Like reinforced steel rods," Evie said, laughing.

Amy and Aadhira smiled at the joke.

"It's nice when they're desperate," Aadhira agreed. "Fun."

"No, Edward gets all whiney," Evie said. "*Please can I jerk off? Please can I cum?*" She motioned to him with the wanker sign and shook her head.

"Did you know Kurt was dirty when you appointed him?" Amy asked Katie.

Kurt caught his breath as the conversation switched to him.

"Of course," the Russian replied.

"I still can't believe you fed on him," Aadhira remarked.

Evie stared at Kurt. "Urgh," she said, and shivered. "Nasty."

"Evie," Aadhira replied. "You're always feeding on them!"

"Yeah, well, when I'm hungry I want to eat," Evie stated.

"How did he taste?" Aadhira asked Katie.

"Not nice," Katie answered. "I had to feed properly to replenish myself."

"Did you go back to that devout Christian?" Aadhira queried.

"I liked that Muslim," Evie said. "He was hot."

Aadhira screwed up her nose. "Not for me."

"He was a Buddhist," Katie advised.

"Oooh," Evie moaned. "A hot Buddhist."

"He was, too." Katie grinned.

"Did you see what happened to his fiancée?" Aadhira asked.

"He's telling the truth," Katie replied. "She did go missing. She lost her baby."

All eyes fell on Kurt, whose jaw clenched and hands tightened into white knuckled fists. "Don't go there," he warned, through gritted teeth.

Katie's brow descended like storm clouds falling upon the landscape of her face. Her mouth opened, a cave marked by sharp fangs. "You don't go there," she warned. "You calm yourself." She took a long, nasally breath and spoke again, her tone softer, empathic, "Calm yourself."

Kurt closed his eyes. The image of his daughter, Lotte, appeared, clutching his forefinger. She smiled and giggled, then coughed. Kurt took a long lung-filling breath and let it all out. His eyes opened. The tears repressed. His anger subsided.

"Aw, poor woman," Aadhira said.

"Like you care," Evie declared.

"Piss off. I would've had a baby if I were still human," Aadhira responded.

"He's dirty, Katie," Evie said, and screwed up her nose. "You need to clean him."

"I will cleanse him properly later," Katie said.

Cleanse me? What the hell does that mean?

"He'll be better when he doesn't taste like sour milk," Amy commented.

"Tragedy does that, doesn't it, Addy?" Evie said. "Makes the blood go off."

"Shut up," Aadhira retorted. "That was a long time ago."

"You're a lucky boy," Evie said. "Katie's going to wank the shit out of you, then you'll not give a damn about your ex. When she's finished, all you'll want to do is serve your new mistress."

"You're scaring him, Evie," Aadhira admonished.

"What? And you don't?" Evie challenged. She leant over the back of her chair to face Kurt again. "You're not scared, are you? She's got you in her web, Kurt, and you're never going to get out. Cock-locked forever."

Kurt swallowed, hoping Evie's words were offered purely for a reaction. "I just want to know what happened to my fiancée, Miss," he said. Despite his bravado, he felt worried. "May I ask, who's Meghan?"

"No," Katie said. "You may not."

"Poor boy," Aadhira said. "He looks terrified now."

"He should be. We're vampires," Evie said. "They should all be shit scared, shouldn't you, Edward?"

"Yes, Miss," her server replied.

"You know your place, don't you?"

"Yes, Miss," he affirmed.

"And Stefan," Evie said. "What a hot piece of cock he is."

"Evie, enough," Amy said. "Kurt, a cleansing eradicates the demons of your past. It is something, should they need it, that all pets and servers go through. You, because of your loss, will benefit from it."

"May I speak freely, Miss?" Kurt asked.

Amy looked across at Katie.

"Go on," Katie instructed.

"If you could tell me what you know, that would do a lot to eradicate the demons of my past, as Miss Amy put it," Kurt said.

"He's so desperate to know," Evie laughed.

"Your fiancée, Kurt, was so overwhelmed by the party that Katie held for me, that she wanted more," Amy said. "Her old life was dead to her."

Evie nodded. "Yeah, she was a royal pain in the ass. Little Miss Whiney. Even getting her pussy licked by a tongue wasn't enough to shut her up."

"A tongue, Miss?" Kurt asked.

"A pet, sometimes a boy, usually a girl, whose sole job is to lick pussy." Evie smiled mischievously.

Kurt froze at the thought of Tanya giving herself over to these women.

"She was lured by a sister called Meghan," Amy continued.

"Yeah, she's one of Chloe's sluts," Evie said loudly. "You don't want to get involved with her. She's a total bitch."

"That is all we know," Amy said. "Meghan may have taken your fiancée as a pet, she may even have turned her, but what is certain, and I suspect that you sense this already, she has gone from your life."

"Where do I find her?" Kurt asked.

"Enough," Katie said, putting an instant stop to his pursuit of answers. "Take our plates."

"I would stop looking for her, Kurt, before you get hurt," Amy warned.

"Kurt, take our plates," Katie insisted.

The four vampires waited expectantly for Katie's server to do as his mistress commanded.

"Please, Miss," he pursued. "If you know where she is or where Meghan is, please tell me."

Four blank faces returned his request with silence.

Stefan and Edward set to quietly removing their plates. Kurt watched for a few moments longer, hoping that one of the sisters might add something extra. A morsel of information that would offer a new trail. When none came, Stefan whispered, "Come on. You may find out more later."

Swearing internally, Kurt heaved a deep and heavy sigh and picked up a plate. He wanted to throw it against the wall, but instead took it with him from the room, his fingers locked diametrically over the furnace-fired crockery. With the two servers taking the lead, they cleared the table and returned to the kitchen where Cook Margarita was cursing their lack of urgency as she dished up the main course. She slapped each backside as the boys left, adeptly catching them with her trusty tea towel. Stefan jumped and grinned while her encouragement added impetus to Edward, who sped up in an attempt to avoid another slap. Kurt received two impacts, one of which smarted his backside sharply. He barely noticed either and staggered back to the room where the sisters had fallen silent. The men set down their next course, Stefan went to Amy, Edward placed one in front of Evie and another for Aadhira, while a dazed Kurt set down the last for Katie. He took his position behind his mistress, standing by the wall, half-listening to their conversation.

"God, Katie, you're new server's a dull one," Evie commented.

"I said he needs cleansing," Katie retorted.

"I didn't like my last one," Aadhira stated.

"Addy didn't like him so much that she killed him," Evie laughed.

"I may have a new one soon," Aadhira said, cutting a small portion of meat. "And I didn't kill him, Evie."

"He killed himself because you edged him until he couldn't take any more," Evie said.

"Evie, will you..." Aadhira began.

"We all know what happened, Evie," Amy said, cutting Aadhira off.

"I couldn't exist without Edward," Evie continued. "I don't know how you manage without one. They go with the lifestyle."

"You have to learn to survive without," Aadhira stated.

"Aadhira is right," Amy agreed. "Not all of us need to have a naked man about the house."

"Don't we?" Evie challenged. "We are what we are. They are what they are. They should be naked. They should serve us. Too many years of women serving them."

"True," Katie agreed.

"Don't we all want one, or ten?" Evie suggested.

"Ten can become a headache," Amy noted.

"Edward has been with me since he left the street," Evie said. "He didn't have anything when he came to me. Now he has everything he wants, don't you?"

"Yes, Miss," Edward said, sounding like a robot.

"I don't really want the hassle of training another one," Aadhira confessed.

"It's no hassle," Evie said. "You know that. You lock his dick up and he's 90% trained. The rest is just fluff."

"Where are all the blood slaves you promised?" Aadhira asked Katie, flipping the conversation to another subject.

"I told her not to bother," Amy said.

"Why? I thought we were trying out some new ones?"

"Because I had a better idea, Aadhira," Amy replied.

The slim vampire frowned. "We're not cleansing Katie's new server are we?"

"No," Amy said. She leaned forward and dropped her voice as if sharing a secret, "I want us to try a communion."

"Communion?" Evie repeated.

"We didn't bring any pets," Evie said.

"You don't have any pets left, do you, Evie?" Katie asked.

"Katie has instructed Emma to serve as the tongue," Amy advised.

"And who's going to be the primary?" Evie asked.

"Aadhira," Amy replied, staring at the sister.

"Me?" Aadhira enquired.

"Is this going to work?" Evie wondered. "Or is it going to be another dead circle, like last time?"

"I enjoyed it," Katie said.

"That's because your pet licked your pussy," Evie asserted. "The rest of us just sat and watched."

"There's only one way to find out," Amy advised.

"After dinner then?" Evie suggested.

"Of course, we don't want to waste Cook Margarita's beautiful food," Amy replied.

They finished their main course and waited for the servers to bring dessert, opting for drinks after their communion.

"Your server's heart centre's throbbing," Aadhira stated, staring at Kurt's chest.

"Just like his dick later on," Evie said and laughed. "He's all pent up with nowhere to put that umph. I hope you don't get turned on by girl-on-girl, Kurt."

Kurt's teeth tightened beneath his closed jaw.

"Go tell Emma we are ready," Katie said to him.

"Yes, Miss," he replied automatically. "Do you know where she is?"

"That's your job," Katie hissed.

Kurt bowed and left to find her.

Chapter Eleven

Emma wasn't far away, having taken up temporary residence in the library and lost herself in an old book. "Katie wants you," Kurt said.

"You alright?" she asked, perking up at his arrival.

"Not really," he replied, trying to soothe away the strain that dominated his face.

"They can be a bit intense," Emma said.

"A bit intense?" Kurt shook his head. "They're awful. I hate them. Why the hell won't they just tell me what happened to her? All they've said is that Tanya wanted to be turned and ended up with someone called Meghan."

"Meghan?"

"Do you know her?" he asked, barely able to contain his anger and frustration.

"I only know *of* her. Meghan is Chloe's daughter. You don't want to mess with Chloe, or Meghan, they're dangerous – scary dangerous. Come on," she said, closing the book and getting up. "I'd give you a hug, but Katie won't want to be kept waiting. Just put it out of your mind. Or at least try to."

"Wait," he said. "At least tell me where I can find her."

"Kurt, if Tanya's with Meghan, you'd better let her go," Emma advised.

"What? Why?"

"I just told you, because she's dangerous."

Kurt shook his head. "Emma, I have to know. Please. Help me."

"Okay," Emma said. "I'll do what I can. Is there anything else I need to know?"

"Apparently, Katie's going to cleanse me later on, whatever the hell that is."

"Yes, that's good. It's a healing."

"Healing? If they want to heal me they should just tell me what happened to her." He wiped his eyes as they threatened to shed tears.

"It'll help, I promise. I had it done myself," Emma said.

"You did?"

"A story for another time," she answered.

"They want you for something called 'communion,'" he replied.

"Right." She paused and stared at him. "You need to cry and you really need to let Tanya go. Especially if she's with Meghan and Chloe, besides, once you've been here for a while, you'll barely remember your old life. Now, come on." She led the way back to the dining room where the remaining servers had cleared the table.

"Emma," Katie said. "Aadhira will be the primary tonight."

"Yes, Miss," Emma replied. Kurt positioned himself beside the other two servers against a wall. His jaw clenched. Fists tightly squeezed behind his back.

"You know what to do," Katie advised.

"Yeah," Evie said, still smiling. "Go taste Aadhira's dessert."

Obediently, Emma dropped to the floor and crawled beneath the table.

Aadhira edged her chair away from the table, pulled the folds of her skirt up to rest on her thighs, and parted her legs.

"Right, hold hands," Amy instructed, placing hers on the table. The four vampires closed their eyes and formed a circle of hands as Emma nestled between Aadhira's legs. She planted the first kiss on her calf, pressing lips over smooth flesh. Swapping from one side to the other. Step-by-step she climbed upwards and inwards.

"Aadhira," Amy said. "You are the conduit; we'll tap into what you are feeling."

"I feel nice," Aadhira replied.

"I can sense her," Evie said, focusing on the vibrating sensations she was receiving through her hands. "Emma has the softest lips."

"Yes," Katie murmured.

"Higher," Amy directed.

Emma's lips swept over Aadhira's knee, landing with delicate kisses on her skin. Gradually she teased her way upwards, dancing over the plain of the vampire's thigh before sweeping in the direction of her shaven mound. Her first contact was a ghost of a touch, tentative and light, gone as soon as it had landed. Another came and went, equal in its fleeting stimulation.

"She's good," Evie commented.

"Shh," Katie hushed.

Emma's mouth danced around Aadhira's pussy. Switching from side to side until she slipped between her lips. Her tongue tentatively stroking around the top of Aadhira's slit.

"God, she's frustrating," Evie murmured. Her hand tightened on the others as Emma's tongue lightly circled Aadhira's clit.

"Yes," Amy sighed.

Aadhira thrust her hips forward, forcing herself against Emma's face. The blonde pet steadied her movements and gently pressed the sister back into her seat. Her lips locked over Aadhira's clit, tugged on it and released. Aadhira's hands tightened on Amy and Evie. Emma's tongue resumed its feathery journey, sweeping over her clit in flicking strokes that drew more and more juices from the vampire.

"My panties are soaked," Evie confessed.

"Keep going, Emma," Katie encouraged, parting her legs as if her pet were sat between them.

Emma's tongue ran over Aadhira's slick pussy, lapping eagerly over the hot folds. She surged upwards, devouring her clit with rapid bursts. Aadhira's legs stretched wider and her fingers clinched her sister's hands. The tidal wave of arousal burst forth from her belly, shooting orgasmic tremors through her slender body.

The sensual pleasure swept through the sisters, exploding like starlight into waves of luminous ecstasy that breached over their bodies. Moans and gasps filled the room as the four vampires were consumed by their synchronised orgasms.

Aadhira was the first to pull herself free. She pushed herself away from the table and Emma, who crawled forth, wiping her mouth with fingers that she licked clean.

"I told you," Amy said, when they had all recovered. "We can use this technique on pets."

"If they are psychic," Evie noted.

"Yes, of course, Evie," Amy agreed. "The point is, we can use it for generating and sharing energy, for rites and for pleasure."

"I'll go with the pleasure," Evie said, smiling at Aadhira. "Nice, huh?"

"Amazing," Aadhira agreed.

"Well done, Emma," Amy said. "Katie has trained you perfectly."

"Thank you, Miss Amy," Emma said and curtsied.

"We shall take our coffee in the drawing room," Katie said to Kurt, glancing at her phone. "Go help Cook Margarita. After that take a shower. I want you clean for later. Stefan and Edward can see to our needs. Emma, go and get ready."

"Later?" Kurt asked, aware that she was referring to the cleansing.

Evie tutted. Edward hurried to her chair as she got up. "No manners. It's Miss Katie to you, you tosser."

Kurt grimaced. *Fuck you,* he thought.

"He'll see," Katie said. Kurt stepped behind her and pulled her chair out as she also stood.

"That's if he's not crying," Evie chuckled. "We all know what you're going to do, Katie."

Crying, Kurt thought, as the anger in his belly tightened into a Gordian knot. *You bitches.*

"Everyone except Kurt knows what to do," Aadhira noted.

"Don't scare the boy," Amy advised.

"Don't worry," Katie said, resting a gentle hand on his shoulder, "he will thank me afterwards."

Evie laughed. "But not during."

Kurt took a long, slow breath and opened his mouth to speak. "I need to know—"

"Not now, Kurt," Amy said, cutting him off. "Your night is not over yet. Katie will answer your questions in her own time. You must learn patience."

Chapter Twelve

"Give him a chance," Emma soothed, watching a red-faced Kurt envelop the tip of his shaft with his fingers. They ran back and forth, stimulating the swollen glans. "I don't think he's ever done anything like this before."

Kurt's muscles tensed as he stared at the attractive pet from his kneeling position. Her transformation was startling: her natural blonde curls had been dyed jet black and combed into severe lines that hung to her shoulders and framed her pretty face. Slashes of eyeliner stabbed horizontally like sharp daggers above sockets painted violet. The comfortable laziness of her girl-next-door outfit had been usurped by a goth look. The plump curve of her breasts peeked out from below a tiny crop top, that also exposed a studded navel and a flower tattoo that wound its way down her left side, over her hip, disappearing into the top of her lace up leggings. A pair of Dr Martens, chained around the heel, matched the studded choker around her neck. It was connected to a leash that her vampire mistress held in her hand.

Katie shook her head. "*Njet*! *Mne ne nravitsya*. He's whining. He needs to prove he has self-discipline and stamina. He is showing neither. He does as I say or I will turn him into a blood slave."

Kurt forced himself to speak between gritted teeth. "I'm sorry, Miss," he began, trembling as his fingers worked back and forth over the tip of his swollen cock. "I'll try to last." He forced his mind to think of something bland; something that would take his mind to an innocuously dull place. His gaze dropped to the floor. He traced the polished wooden panels, identifying knots and lines in the grains of wood.

"He will not last," Katie said from her throne. Like Emma, her outfit was black: leather trousers with thigh-high boots, a bodice bound tight around her waist and cupping her breasts, between which his key hung. Her skin looked pale, like grey-white snow coating a landscape trapped beneath a blanket of dark cloud. Her tight lips relaxed, slipping into a half smile, as though she were reluctant to release her feelings of irritation and contempt. It added to the nervous vulnerability that was threatening to consume him.

His voice tightened as he spoke. "I will. It's just..." His top lip folded between his teeth as he forced himself to control the deep urge to satisfy his desires, to abandon the forced discipline, grab his dick tightly and jerk himself to an exploding orgasm. "It's... very... hard... to keep... going."

Emma grinned, delighted at his predicament. "Aw, poor boy."

"Shh," Katie snapped, tugging the lead attached to Emma's choker. It jolted the reborn goth back against the legs of the throne.

"I think he needs more oil," Emma suggested.

Katie's smile exorcised the austerity from her face. "He may have signed the contract, but if he wishes to serve me, he has a lot to prove."

Kurt stared back at her and cursed himself for doing so. He was already aroused, he didn't need more stimulation. The warm glow of the wall lights gleamed over her long leather boots. He had cleaned them that afternoon, along with a dozen or so more, and now she was wearing them while he edged himself at her pleasure.

"He just needs to learn some self-control," Emma soothed.

"He's not dead, is he?" Katie snapped.

Emma laughed. "He needs oil. He'll rub himself raw."

"Go on then," Katie said, releasing Emma's chain.

"Thank you," Kurt said, stopping as Emma got up. He tried to compose himself. There was no doubt he felt alive, utterly, totally invigorated by the self-stimulation. Touching a place that he had never experienced. It was simultaneously beautiful and torturous.

"I didn't tell you to stop," Katie snapped. "You have been given an instruction, now carry it out. If you cannot..."

"I'm sorry," Kurt said. "I'm so horny, Miss."

"Aw, poor boy," Emma said, giggling as she approached. Her smile faded as she picked up the bottle that had been set beside the padlock and chastity cage at his side. "If you want the honour of serving Miss Katie, you'd better listen, boy." Her eyes flashed, invigorated by Kurt's swollen predicament. She gave the bottle a deliberately provocative shake as though she were jerking it off. "And obey."

Kurt caught his breath. "I'm... trying."

"*Prodolzhay*," Katie said.

"Continue," Emma translated, moving closer.

Kurt took a deep breath and wet his lips. He looked tense, as though he were about to cry. "Please..." His head tilted back, his gaze locked on the ceiling. His wrist bent back towards himself, fingers outstretched and slipping around his helmet.

"Here," Emma said, flipping the lid and holding the bottle over his swollen cock.

"*Ostanovis*!" Katie barked.

"Stop!" Emma commanded. "Stop. It's okay." Her words were soft and motherly. "Move your hand."

Momentarily relieved, Kurt shook his arm in an attempt to circulate the blood, then rested it at his side. His hard-on felt like tempered steel.

Emma tipped the bottle further, squeezing a trail of clear liquid onto his phallus.

"Hurry up," Katie said.

"Rub it in," Emma whispered.

"Oh God." He gasped as Emma lingered beside him and watched as he massaged his swollen cock until it gleamed.

"Continue!" Katie said.

"Please, may I rest, Miss?" he pressed.

"Continue!" Katie commanded.

"I'd do what she says," Emma advised. There was a twinkle in her eyes as his extended fingers slid back over the tip of his erection. She put the bottle down.

Kurt's upper body bent forward in response to the pulsing heat of his cock. The need to stroke himself was magnetic, a gravity field that he fought against. It shot arrows of pleasure through his body, forcing his teeth to clamp shut and his breath into long, slow gasps.

"Concentrate," Emma whispered.

"Emma," Katie said.

The blonde-turned-goth skipped back to her place at her mistress's feet. Katie took her leash once more and wrapped it around her wrist.

"Look at me," Katie instructed, watching Kurt's back arch as his fingers drove down over the head of his cock.

Obediently, the server focused on the Russian vampire.

"Good boy," Emma praised.

Katie stroked the top of Emma's head. "Now."

Kurt hesitated, uncertain of the instruction. "Miss?"

"Don't stop," Emma instructed. "Keep going."

Kurt's fingers slipped over the mushroom head, stopping at the first knuckle, then withdrawing to repeat the process. Back and forth they pistoned over his prick with a slow, steady motion that drew him closer and closer to the edge of orgasm.

"Close your eyes," Emma said, getting up again. "Don't stop."

Kurt obeyed, pleased to obliterate the image of the two attractive women.

"Imagine a red ball of energy, behind your balls," Emma continued. "It's bright, pulsing and hot. Can you feel it?"

Kurt frowned.

"Concentrate," Emma reiterated.

"I don't know," Kurt replied.

"Go to him," Katie said.

"Keep trying," Emma instructed, her voice growing louder as she approached. "It's a beautiful red, like a sunset on a tropical island. You see it, feel it, at the base of your spine. It's pulsing and throbbing. Feel that energy, the heat in its centre. Have you got it?"

"I... I think so," Kurt replied, his fingers still working over the tip of his rigid phallus. "Yes. Yes, I can see it."

"Yes," Katie nodded. "More. Concentrate more."

Kurt's brow tightened over his closed eyes.

"Not like that, you fool," Katie sighed.

"Relax," Emma soothed, coming to a halt beside the aroused young man. "Relax." Her meditative instruction eased his tension, and his shoulders dropped a little. The muscles in his arms and legs loosened. "Try again," Emma continued. "This time, make it rotate."

Kurt's hand stopped moving as he visualised the red orb spinning.

"Don't stop," Emma said. "Keep going. Picture it in your mind. When you've got it, watch a line of energy rise to your belly button."

Emma's instruction tempered Kurt's arousal, guiding his inner eye.

"Fuck! Come on!" Katie moaned. "If he can't do this, I'm draining him."

Kurt's muscles tensed once more.

"It's okay," Emma soothed.

His fingers stretched over the fleshy head, flooding his mind and body with the delightful sensations.

"Concentrate. A line of energy rises to your navel."

"I'm so horny," he gasped through gritted teeth. His hand didn't stop. His thighs bulged, his balls sat full and tight beneath his hard prick. "This is too much."

Emma blasted a rapid instruction. "Focus on your belly button. Visualise an orange orb."

Kurt's eyes burst open. "I'm going to cum."

"No cumming!" Emma shouted.

Kurt stared at her. His body shivered, his fingers still driving over the tip of his cock, his legs shaking. "I need to cum. I'm desperate. God, please!"

"No!" Emma shouted, tearing his arm away as his fingers rotated into a fist.

Katie was beside him instantly. She pulled his left arm backwards, took his right from Emma and clasped them both tightly as she slipped in behind him and hauled him into a standing position. His body was hot. Sweat dripped from his strong shoulders, trickled down his back and over the curve of his buttocks. "You're useless," she hissed. Her cool breath trailed over his neck and shoulders. "I should kill you."

"He just needs some training," Emma pacified. She moved closer, nestling against his side and nuzzling up to Katie.

Kurt's heart was racing. His cock twitched, his balls and abdomen thundered as though he'd been punched in the stomach. He felt Katie's fingernails cut into his wrists, her cool breath on his neck. "I'm tired, and I want his energy," she said, nibbling his shoulder.

"I'll guide him," Emma said. "He'll do it, I promise."

"If you don't, Kurt," Katie whispered as she kissed the hot flesh of his neck, "I'll lock that cock up and you'll never, ever cum again."

"He'll do it," Emma reasoned. She stepped in front of him. "Won't you, Kurt?"

"I'm so horny," he gasped, staring at Emma while feeling Katie's body tight behind him.

"Just calm your breathing," Emma offered. "Take slow, deep breaths."

Kurt followed her instruction until she asked him again. "Will you do as Katie asks?"

"Yes, Miss. Can I have some more oil please? I think I understand."

"Good." Releasing him, Katie pinched his backside. She returned to her seat, crossed her legs and sat back, arms on the rests. "Next time, you'll stay locked as you eat my pussy."

"I'll do it, Miss," Kurt replied.

"Here." Emma handed him the bottle, and he poured the oil onto himself, lathered it into the hard flesh and over the head, then placed the bottle on the floor.

"Start again," Emma instructed, resting a hand on his shoulder.

Kurt closed his eyes once more and inhaled sharply through his nostrils. He moistened his mouth and formed a loose tube with his fingers.

"Concentrate," Emma directed. "Fingers on the head only. Imagine the ball of red energy at the base of your spine. Each time your fingers go over the tip of your cock, imagine the ball pulse and throb. As you keep going, feel the energy stream upwards to the orange centre at your belly button. Do you understand?"

"Yes," Kurt replied.

"Good," Emma said, and kissed him on the cheek. She stepped back, watching him as he restarted the process.

He was grunting straight away. "This is too much! This is too much!" he cried, as his fingers glided back and forth over the tip.

"You can do it," Emma encouraged.

"That's better," Katie said, watching the red energy pulse at the base of his spine.

"This is... this is... t-too much," Kurt stammered, rhythmically massaging his glans.

"Orange," Emma said hurriedly. "Just below your belly button. A small orb. Concentrate."

"If you cum it'll be your last time," Katie warned.

Kurt swallowed. His hand remained in place, hips rocking back and forth like a pendulum marking time.

"Orange ball," Emma urged. "You see an orange ball, just below your belly button."

Kurt forced himself to concentrate, forming the orange orb in his mind's eye.

"Good," Katie murmured. "Move on. Next one."

"Another line of energy rises," Emma instructed. "From the orange ball at your navel up through a yellow sphere at your solar plexus, to the centre of your chest. It stops at a green ball."

Images shot through Kurt's mind, frantic images that he battled to contain. "No," he said, shaking his head desperately.

"There," Katie said. "You see her, don't you, Kurt?"

"Yes," he gasped, as the image of Tanya appeared clearly in his mind's eye. She was sad; lost and withered in that old, brown leather armchair by the downstairs window. The armchair that he had come to loathe. That he wanted to burn.

Tears streamed down his cheeks. He felt aged, racked with pain that clung to him like virulent ivy. "I can't do this," he breathed.

"You must," Katie asserted. There was no anger or hatred in her voice, only a fierce determination fed from his emotions. "You must face this."

"I can't," Kurt shouted. The tears hadn't stopped. He dropped to the floor, his cock quivering, his head lost in his hands.

"You have to," Emma said. "You can't stop now. Believe me, I've been there."

"I don't care. I don't want to do this."

"You have to face it," Emma comforted, stroking his back.

"Continue," Katie asserted.

Kurt shook his head.

Chapter Thirteen

Tanya's bag was packed for the party. She looked beautiful in a blue regency gown bought especially for the occasion. Her heels raised her to match Kurt's height. Her make-up was subtle rather than overbearing. Hair freshly cut, nails manicured by her friend at the agency.

It was the first step, Kurt hoped, as he dropped her off at the station, towards a new life for them both.

"Now, follow her," Katie instructed. "Follow your fiancée and see what happened."

Kurt looked at the vampire. His fingers still working his cock. He swallowed, wet his lips again and uncertain of her command, asked, "What happened to her?"

The vampire got up, stepped down from the platform and watched him. "Don't stop."

He shook his head resolutely. His fingers still pistoning against the engorged head of his swollen member. "This is too hard."

"Don't stop," Katie repeated.

"Just concentrate," Emma encouraged.

"I can't."

"You have to finish, Kurt," Katie said. "You are my server, as you have made a contract to me, so I am bound to you."

"I'll cum," Kurt growled. "I'm so horny."

"I told you not to stop," Katie reiterated. Her long boots creaked as she approached; they smelt of homely leather and rich polish. She stopped on the opposite side to Emma. "You are clouded by a dark energy that saps your strength," she said. "I will heal you. Now, close your eyes."

His eyelids descended.

Extravagance was the word for the party that Tanya had organised. The palatial home was of the old British aristocratic tradition. Stone built from the blood and toil of the workers of the empire, be they native to the soil of Britain or imported from conquered territories.

The ballroom was packed with sister vampires, looking striking in their regency gowns and bonnets. Long gloves covered hands and lower arms, while sleeves puffed from the shoulders of their gowns. If the only attendees were sisters, it could have been mistaken for a scene out of a Jane Austen novel, albeit one lacking the opposite sex, yet there were others in addition to the vampires.

Pets wore bloomers and bodices or see-through petticoats. Their dances were scenes of vertical love as they writhed and rubbed against one another to the satisfaction of the watching sisters. Breasts massaged backs. Thighs pushed between thighs, sliding up and down against aroused pussies. Lips found lips. Kisses found cheeks and necks. Hands on breasts, backsides and wet cunts as they danced to the erotic songs sliced together by a beautiful DJ.

Amidst the sapphic cavorting, nude men, their match-fit bodies gleaming from a lathering of oil, ferried trays of drinks and discards to and fro. Every man, of every ethnicity, was a perfected Adonis. Cocks, hardened by tongues, pointed forward as they navigated from room to room.

Tanya's arousal increased at the unhindered indulgence exhibited by the carnality of the flesh.

Amy was centre-stage, a magnificent queen of the underworld. Her jaw painted with a mixture of fresh and dried blood that trailed in branches down her throat and over her breasts, where they disappeared in the blackness of her long, satin gown. Each corset button held a set of tiny keys. They jingled as she moved.

She smiled as Tanya approached. Her seductive blue eyes popped from their black painted sockets, adding a sinister quality as she welcomed Kurt's fiancée. He felt the vampire's warm hand take Tanya's and pull her through the ensemble of naked blood slaves and half-dressed pets, and feeding sisters.

"Thank you," Amy whispered, and kissed Tanya on the cheek.

Tanya smiled and touched her face. Her fingertips red from the sticky blood that the vampire had marked her with.

"I'm going to heal you," Katie said, grabbing the oil, then pouring it over her hand and onto Kurt's erection. "Keep your eyes closed. Emma..."

"Don't fight it," Emma soothed.

Kurt felt her hand on his shoulder. It was a gentle caress, a reassuring touch that she would remain at his side while he faced his demons. He emitted a sharp gasp as Katie's cool fingers slipped over the tip of his cock. Smooth and well-lubricated they glided over him, her long fingernails tentatively scraping against his shaft as she rubbed his head. Ever-so-slowly, she picked up a rhythm.

"Return to the green centre," Emma said. "See it in the middle of your chest. Over your heart. It's wounded. It is time for it to be healed."

Kurt felt a wall inside his mind fracture as the river of thoughts and feelings, dammed by his inability to speak to Tanya, flooded into his being. From the chaos that erupted in his mind and heart he shot back to the party and the experience of his fiancée.

Tanya wanted more. Like a would-be junkie lured to greater pleasures by a brief hit. Amy's bloody kiss, platonic in its gesture, had grounded the realness of the world she had unwittingly orchestrated.

In the planning stage, servers had been called waiters. Pets were dancers. Tongues, fans. Acronyms and euphemisms obscured a reality that Tanya only realised once the party had begun.

She had been free to leave, to accept the pretense that it was a LARPING group, roleplaying as vampires, pretending to be something they were not. Indulging in fetish play that some might find extreme and others might want to join. Yet she had remained.

Overwhelmed by the self-assured confidence of the sisters, she had wanted more. She needed it. Wherever she looked couples and groups indulged in the great erotic dance of life. Tongues teased their way around sodden pussies or savoured the hard prick of a blood slave. Outstretched arms formed crosses from which sisters fed; open wrists sharing the red wine of communion.

Visions of handsome, naked men, whose tight backsides barely jiggled as they hurried to waiting women who wanted an equal measure of refill and entertainment.

Tanya found herself watching from the sidelines, her thighs tight together. Her underwear sodden by her juices as she watched a group of men serve a table of severe looking sisters.

"Are you Tanya?" a woman asked, beckoning her over.

Tanya smiled.

"Are you?" she repeated in a softer tone.

"Yes."

"Come here."

Cautiously, Tanya approached the seated vampire.

"Hello," Tanya said, studying the woman. She had a square face with a sharp nose and a pointed chin, yet possessed a glowing beauty that was quite mesmerising. Her blonde hair snapped in a straight line above her neck. Her gaseous blue eyes were like a collapsed star exhibiting two hypnotically black dots in their centres. "Are you responsible for this?"

"Responsible?" Tanya repeated, unable to draw her eyes from the vampire's pin-pointed orbs.

"Are you?"

"I planned it, yes," Tanya admitted.

"It's nice to dress up," the woman said, plucking the fabric of her gown. "Come sit with us." Still seated, she offered Tanya her hand. "I'm Meghan."

Her heart pounding, Tanya accepted. The vampire slipped her fingers into Tanya's, folding over the knuckle and squeezing her gently. She pulled her closer where another vampire, severe in her gaze, beautiful in her features, watched her.

Meghan was up and guiding Tanya into the vacant seat in a blur. She slid in beside her, closing the space and sealing Tanya in. "I have a tongue for you," she announced. Her hand rested on Tanya's thigh and pulled it open.

Tanya's legs stiffened.

"What are you afraid of?" Meghan asked, parting her own legs. A head of long brown hair appeared. The woman, a thirty-something Caucasian, smiled as she delved deep between Meghan's thighs.

Tanya took a sharp but deep breath, as hands ran over her legs. Another woman, identical to the first, smiled and waited for her legs to widen.

"You want to keep that hell you are carrying around with you all night?" Meghan asked. "Or enjoy this magnificent evening?"

Tanya swallowed and relaxed. The tongue separated her legs and shuffled forward.

Kurt's heart fluttered beneath the overwhelming tide of emotion. He sensed Katie's fingers perpetually fucking the head of his cock, Emma's hand gently stroking his shoulder. "Let it out," she whispered.

"I can see her," he said. "She's there, with Meghan."

"Good," Emma said. "Concentrate."

Kurt watched as Tanya received her first orgasm from the tongue. There were more to follow, three by the time the night was out. As if their infernal magic had worked its way into her heart, his fiancée was begging Meghan to take her with her by night's end.

"Please," Tanya begged. She dropped, to her knees, pleading to be freed from a life that she had come to hate. "I need this," she declared. "Meghan. Please. I can't go back. I can't face him anymore. I just can't."

"She's already annoying," the vampire from the north declared.

Meghan gave her friend a hug. "I'm going to take her, Chloe," she confided.

"Good luck," the vampire replied. "She's clingy."

"Maybe she should become my tongue," Meghan smiled, exposing her fangs. Her friend disappeared, leaving Meghan and Tanya alone.

"Fine, you can be my pet," Meghan said.

"Thank you," Tanya said, tears drawing stain lines down her cheeks.

The vampire kissed her passionately, pressing soft flat lips against Tanya's. Weaving her tongue over her newly accepted pet. Her hands squeezed Tanya's backside as Meghan's small breasts squashed against Tanya's larger curves.

When she was done and Tanya was reeling from the amorous coupling, she released her. "I will come for you," she said. "Be ready. Bring nothing. Leave everything."

"She made a pact," Kurt breathed. "She made a deal with Meghan. She wanted to go with her." His chest hurt. His cock throbbed. His stomach knotted at the betrayal.

"Don't stop," Emma said.

Kurt felt Katie's fingers cupping the top of his shaft as they drew back and forth.

"Keep going. Keep concentrating," Emma urged.

"Oh my god," Kurt gasped.

He watched as the image switched from party to home. He was sitting in the kitchen when she returned. "How was it?" he asked, as she practically danced into the house. So full of life that she didn't want to sleep. Didn't want to sit in her old leather chair nor hold the cushion that had acted as a surrogate baby. She was full of vitality. A shot of life had been injected into her.

"A resounding success," she replied, draping her arms around his shoulders. Her lips found his neck. Her hands wound around and squeezed his backside, forcing his hips into hers. She rubbed herself against him. Grinding him to hardness. A hardness that she dropped to her knees to accommodate. Slowly, teasingly, staring up at him with a wicked look in her eye. Mischievous as her mouth opened seductively. She stretched the elastic of his joggers from his waist and glanced down at the placid length that was hiding beneath the material. She delved in, catching her prize, pulling his joggers lower as she pulled him towards her mouth...

Kurt opened his eyes. Katie was standing before him, looking strong and powerful and potent, despite the coolness to her grip. Her fingers slid back and forth over his tip, driving the energy that had exposed a painful knowledge.

"Close your eyes, Kurt," Emma soothed. "Close your eyes."

His eyelids closed, casting him into the haunting shadows of memory lane.

Their love making lasted the night. Her body transformed from the cold, rigid melancholic tomb of a fiancée to a nubile lover, pregnant with lust, insatiable in her desire. He took her three times that night. She exploded each time in orgasms that grew ever wilder, ever more passionate, ever more unbounded. They slept as the sun birthed a new day. Lost in each others arms. When he awoke, he made coffee and sat in her old, brown armchair thanking God, the cosmos, everything and anything that she had come back to him. He made brunch, took it to her and they made love once more before they showered.

"I want a new life with you," he said. "We can try again. We'll have another; one, two, three, I don't mind, as long as you're happy and you're by my side."

Her non-committal answers eventually faded into silence.

"We'll be more careful next time and besides, the trying is always the fun bit." He grinned.

She avoided his glance. Her distant gaze only briefly touching his before she looked away. She was already done, Kurt realised, watching the memory replay. It was already over.

"Tanya," Kurt called, feeling his heart break at the vision before him.

"Keep going," Emma whispered. "Keep going."

Katie's torturous fingers pumped his swollen member. His body was shaking. His hips thrusting against her. His engorged phallus almost burning against the stimulation of her cool hand.

Kurt watched his past self awaken the following night. Something inside him was already certain of the absence that awaited his presence. His bare feet padded down the stairs as a cool breeze delineated the contours of his body from the open front door. He left it untouched as he made his way to the seat of her consolation.

His voice was quiet at first, a question that probed gently rather than an urgent demand for acknowledgement. "Tanya?" Unanswered, its repetition grew bolder, more assertive. "Tanya?"

The living room was a rainbow of shadows. Pitch in places, shaded in deep patches of dark grey in others. The miserable armchair waited empty like an open grave. Her comfort cushion, a broken gravestone cast upon the dead floor of their family home.

Kurt continued his search through the house, despairing as each room increased his need for her. He ran outside, shouting her name in the hope that she was there, silently waiting for him. She would smile and hug him. Kiss him and grab his hand. They would run back into the house, up the stairs to the bedroom where they would dive onto the bed, lost in one another as they made love again.

But Tanya was lost. Lost to the empty night. Lost somewhere, be it a mile or a millennia away. Distance or time, it did not matter.

"Where is she?" he asked, opening his eyes and staring at Katie.

"Look," she answered, her fingers still pumping over the head of his cock.

Kurt's eyelids curtained his view of the room, cutting most from his perception, leaving only Katie's hand and body visible as she edged him deeper into his trance.

There was a haze to Tanya's world when his eyes closed, enabling him to refocus. It was a half-light, like viewing her life through an age-scarred window.

He tracked her movements like a hellhound trailing an astral scent, that took him far from their home to a plush beach house on the Northumberland coast.

He watched as Tanya offered her body and soul to the vampire called Meghan. He shook his head as they made love. It began a one-sided affair as Meghan took his fiancée for her own pleasure. It finished as a dance of sapphic lovers equal in their desire and demands for one another.

"She became her pet," Kurt said, watching his fiancée serve her vampire mistress with finger, lip and tongue. It wrenched open his heart. Inverted his whole world. A steroid induced kick to the balls. A heavy weight punch to the belly. "But not like Emma, more like a slave."

The image faded, replaced by Tanya dressed as a maid, and he watched as his fiancée was humiliated by Meghan and her sisters. Treated like trash. Ignored, rebuked, scorned. When her sisters had gone, Meghan would make love to Tanya again. Apologetic love. Love that pulled back the curtains on Meghan's hard persona. Her sharp features softened beneath the candelight. Her small breasts surged beneath the waves of Tanya's tongue. Her pussy eager for her pet's attention.

When she was alone Tanya broke down again, collapsing into herself, clutching her pillow in her well-furnished bedroom.

Kurt felt her longing. For home, for him. For anything but the hell she could not escape. He watched as a new night unfolded. Meghan's sisters returned, the northern vampire, Chloe, with them. They talked and laughed at the humiliation of the desperate men they had brought to play with. They forced them to masturbate. To edge themselves without cumming. They fed on a few. Forced them all into chastity before they sent them, blue-balled, away to their homes.

"Your fiancée is a server now," Meghan said, as the conversation focused on her pet. "He's sworn to serve that bitch Katie. His dick is locked away and he is kept naked. He left because you abandoned him and so he abandoned you." She laughed.

"Forget him. You are Meghan's pet," Chloe said. "You have no other life unless she allows it."

"I know, Miss," Tanya said, forlornly. Heartbroken, she returned at dawn to her bedroom and cried herself to sleep.

"There is more," Katie said, sliding her fingers back down, over the head of his cock.

"More?" Kurt gasped.

"Watch," Katie advised.

"No," Kurt cried. "No more. No more."

"You must," Katie said.

"I can't! I can't!" Kurt's balls spasmed, shooting white seed from his swollen cock into the palm of Katie's hand. About his physical body, a tsunami of energy erupted. Tears blasted from his eyes, and he fell against her. Shuddering and crying, wanting to be lost in that black cloud once more. Wrapped up and forgotten by the world.

"You should have kept going," Katie said as his orgasm rose and fell.

"There is one last thing you need to do," Emma advised.

"What?" Kurt asked, gasping for breath.

"It's alright," Emma said. "You'll see soon enough."

Epilogue

Kurt parked Katie's car on the drive, killed the engine and sat for a few moments in silence. Katie and Emma, seated in the back, remained thankfully quiet. The place felt melancholy; a lobotomised home. An abandoned hovel amidst the life giving light from the surrounding houses in their cul-de-sac. The front door was closed; darkness awaiting.

When his mental and emotional preparations were complete, he got out, closed the door behind him, and walked steadily towards the front door. His first steps were tentative like a ghost hunter stalking cautiously towards a haunted house.

He opened the door and stared into the emptiness. So many memories hung in the stale air. Their happy moving-in day, followed by fun and frolics as they explored each other's bodies in the different rooms. Things fell into a good and happy routine. Tanya's tales of hip parties for cool people. Kurt's of his eccentric bosses and their carefree attitudes. He remembered her standing in the doorway to the lounge as he arrived home, barely able to contain her excitement as she told him that she was pregnant. So much changed over the following months. A room was decorated. Furniture, bottles, nappies and clothing purchased and stored. Everything was idyllic until their happy future was cast into a black hole.

The familiar hum of the fridge-freezer snapped into life as he entered. His first step felt invasive, turning him into an intruder in his own home. He took a deep, cautious breath and spoke: "Tanya?"

There was no answer. He made his way to the lounge. The furniture was illuminated by the sickly orange of the street lights. Her armchair was empty. Her comfort cushion missing. He didn't navigate the remainder of the ground floor but returned instead to the hallway, where he was drawn to the stairs. He climbed one heavy step at a time.

On the first floor, every door except one was closed. The nursery, prepared but never used, was beside the bathroom and opposite their bedroom.

What am I doing? he thought, dismissing his return as a silly idea.

"You must go home," Katie had told him after he'd emptied himself into her hand. "Then you will be free." She hadn't explained any more and after a sleepless rest, he had accepted her advice.

Tanya, where are you?

Her response was apparent as he stepped into the nursery, answered in the form of her lifeless body. Of her eyes closed to the world. Of her mouth shut to speech. If there had been no dark stain around her, nor pill bottle beside her, he might have mistaken her death for sleep, but her wrists were open and the uncapped bottle was empty. Tanya was dead.

"No," Kurt cried, dropping to the floor and lifting the body of his fiancée into his arms. Panic set in like molten lava running through his veins. He shook her, naively hoping for some reaction. A cough and a splutter, like a drowning victim resuscitated at the last moment. But Tanya's skin was the colour of death. Her body cold like a winter's frost.

The comfort cushion lay beside her, atop that a picture of Kurt, Tanya, and Lotte. He gazed at it as he clutched her body. Gazed at their captured past. The blast of happiness that had been washed away by the bleak reality of a cruel world.

"Kurt." It was Katie's voice. She only spoke once, waited for him to resolve his mourning and shed his fragile tears.

"She only wanted a baby," he choked. "Was that too much to ask?"

Katie's silence fell upon the nursery.

He glanced over his shoulder and stared at the vampire. "What do I do now?"

"Come with me, Kurt," she soothed. "You accepted me as your goddess. Take my hand and walk with me into the darkness."

THE END

Don't miss out!

Visit the website below and you can sign up to receive emails whenever PGDevlim publishes a new book. There's no charge and no obligation.

https://books2read.com/r/B-A-HPZI-DZVGC

BOOKS 2 READ

Connecting independent readers to independent writers.

Did you love *Katie's Server*? Then you should read *Vampire's Key*[1] by PG DEVLIM!

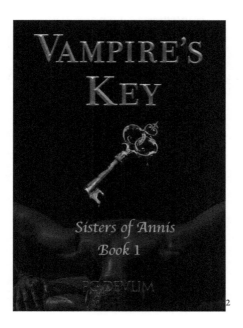

Dominant Female Vampires!

On a cold winters morning Lilly Armitage ventured down a dark alley in search of answers. She had no idea of what lay ahead, of the darkness and delight the powerful Sisters of Annis would show her. Nor of the overwhelming eroticism of their nightclub The Countess, where handsome, naked males served dominant female vampires.

Yet for all the decadent and empowering sensuality, Lilly would soon find herself caught in the middle of a centuries old conflict that threatened the very existence of the world she had embraced.

---

1. https://books2read.com/u/b5Qn1A

2. https://books2read.com/u/b5Qn1A

Uncertain who to trust and with a violent boyfriend hunting her down, Lilly was drawn deeper and deeper into a battle she wasn't certain she would even survive.

An excerpt from Vampire's Key:

'The women — vampires she reckoned — were dressed in different outfits: some in long gowns, others in jeans and t-shirts, while others wore transparent jumpsuits that exposed more flesh than they covered, or stylishly low cut, mini dresses of lace, leather or latex. But the men... the men were all naked, as far as she could tell.'

The Vampire's Key is the first book in the Sisters of Annis series. Combining dominant, keyholding female vampires with a quest that ventures beyond the known world. It is a power-hungry, energy dripping journey into a dark world that may just leave you wishing for that tenuous bite from a strange and beautiful creature on a cold, dark winters night.

"The writing style hooks you immediately!"
"I would highly recommend this book to anyone."
"His style of writing is catchy, entertaining and to the point."
"Excellent twist."
"The writer immerses you in this dark and tantalising world."
"Characters that I really became invested in."
"The erotic scenes were great."

Unveiling the secretive world of powerful and decadent female vampires, this is a book that will leave you desperate for more...

Don't miss out on this fast-paced erotic vampire book!
Buy Now!
Read more at https://pgdevlim.wixsite.com/pgdevlim

Also by PGDevlim

Sisters of Annis Novellas
Katie's Server

Milton Keynes UK
Ingram Content Group UK Ltd.
UKHW010443220424
441503UK00001B/13